The Church of TV as God

THE NEW BIZARRO AUTHOR SERIES

PRESENTS

The Church of TV as God

DANIEL VLASATY

Eraserhead Press
Portland, OR

ERASERHEAD PRESS
205 NE BRYANT
PORTLAND, OR 97211

WWW.ERASERHEADPRESS.COM

ISBN: 1-62105-119-6

Copyright © Daniel Vlasaty

Cover art copyright © Stephen King

Printed in the USA.

Editor's Note

I have a thing for books that include social commentary. I have a thing for books that are about characters I want to believe in, sympathize with and love. I have a thing for books that are fun, incredibly entertaining and have a lot of weird elements. I especially have a thing for books with talking dogs.

Enter Daniel Vlasaty.

His first published book, *The Church of TV as God,* has all of these things, and more. How could I not want to work on this book?

Besides, Daniel is fabulous. He's a consummate professional who produced a fabulous book that was so easy for the reader and editor in me to say yes to, right off the bat.

I can't wait to see what else Daniel writes that I'll want to say, "YES!" to.

I'm happy to present Daniel Vlasaty's book to you as part of the New Bizarro Author Series. This is this author's first book! The NBAS strives to bring new voices in bizarro fiction to our readers. It serves as an opportunity to introduce you to new writers, and to introduce them into the world of being an author. Eraserhead Press is happy to bring new, weird voices to you in the hopes that these authors will prove themselves to be strong members of the bizarro community and continue to entertain you for years to come. The publishing of this book marks the beginning of a one year proving period. Please help support our NBAS writers in their endeavors by telling your friends about their cool new books. This book you hold is only one of several hundred that must be sold in order for this author to continue on his path. We hope you help him along as best as you can. Thank you.

~Spike Marlowe

For Ashley, my wife and best friend.

Part One: The Savior

They are sitting in a room made of TVs. The walls are hundreds of TVs stacked on top of each other, all tuned to different channels, displaying different images. All with the sound muted. It is a church. The Church of TV as God.

The parishioners, dressed in gray robes with shaved heads, sit on TV sets, screens flickering against their pale legs. The man in white stands up at the front, on the sanctuary, a shadow against the flat screen TV altar. "Yes, my followers, my friends, the prophecies are correct," he says. "I can feel it... deep in my bones. The chosen one shall soon join us. He will show himself to us and lead us into salvation. He will bring about the second coming of The Great TV in the Sky. Can you feel it, my friends?" He holds his arms up over his head, waiting for confirmation from his congregation.

They all nod in agreement. They are quiet today, waiting for the man in white to tell them what to do, how to feel. An older woman stands up, her TV-seat rocking as her weight shifts. She throws her hands in the air and starts shaking in the aisle, channeling The Great TV in the Sky. "Oh," she says, twitching, "oh, Great TV... I can *feel* it!" She falls to the ground, on top of the hundreds of extension cords running there, connecting all the TVs. She flops around like a dying fish. "Oh, oh. He's coming... coming." She faints from exhaustion. She has been with the church since the very beginning. She is a true believer in The Great

9

TV in the Sky. She is also very much in love with the man in white. More than anyone else in The Church of TV as God.

The congregation watches her on the floor. Her legs continue to twitch. "Will someone please help Margaret back to her room?" the man in white says. Three young boys rush forward to help, willing to do anything to please the man in white.

The boys pick Margaret up. She comes to just enough to say, "He's coming," once again. She adds, "Soon," and as she is led from the room all the TVs go black at the same time. There is the static hiss that they have all come to know and love. The screens around them flicker, and the image of a man with a glowing face comes into focus.

Jeremy is turning into a TV. The skin around his eyes glows the cold blue of a TV playing in a dark room. His jaw is becoming more square. He can feel what he thinks are antennas starting to poke out of his scalp, still buried under his thick black hair. This is just the beginning. Soon the skin on his face will harden into the glass of a screen. He knows this is happening, and there is nothing he can do about it. It has happened to his father and his grandfather and his great-grandfather. And so on. All the men in Jeremy's family, as far back as their history can be traced, have turned into TVs. It is some kind of disease, a curse—no one knows because no one talks about it. Better to ignore the things you can't explain.

Jeremy wakes up with that fuzzy feeling floating around in his head. He is starting to get used to it, but he is not sure if he really wants to. This feeling is the beginning of the end for him. He remembers his father explaining this feeling to him when he started to transform. He shakes it out of his mind, moves over to the window, and fills his head with the last of the afternoon's warmth instead. Jeremy has been working the night shift lately and his body is still not quite used to this, going to bed when it is getting light, waking to darkness.

He works as a security guard at an appliance cemetery. It is stupid and boring and easy and the pay is shit. He hates it. But a job is a job. The irony of the fact that *he* works at an appliance cemetery is not lost on him.

The appliance cemetery is connected to the normal, people cemetery. Not many people are even aware it exists. It just looks like another section of buried bodies, gravestones, perfectly manicured lawns, flowers. But once you cross the threshold you start to notice things are a bit off about it. The gravestones give it away. They are refrigerators and stoves and microwaves and furnaces cut from polished stones instead of crosses and angels. They have engravings like: *You were a good fridge—you kept my beer cold* and *Your memory will live on in every meal we cook on our new stove.*

Jeremy isn't sure why anyone would want to bury an appliance. He thinks it is an expensive way to throw the thing in the garbage. But people get sentimental about all kinds of crap—it is not his place to judge.

Jeremy makes his rounds. The cemetery is closed to visitors after dark. His shift is slow and boring as usual, until he hears something echoing around the statues of air conditioning units and space heaters. Statues and gravestones far nicer than anything he will be buried with. Flashlight beams slice through the darkness. He sneaks closer to the voices and lights, hides behind a six-foot tall statue of a microwave oven atop a burning volcano. He sees that it is a group of kids, three of them, maybe mid-teens. Grave robbers. They are huddled around a recently buried plot, digging into the dirt with small shovels.

This is an on-going problem for the appliance cemetery. People digging up the appliances to sell the parts for scraps. Or to fix up and use themselves.

Jeremy steps out from behind the statue. The kids are too busy with their digging to notice him until he is directly behind them, the light from his glowing face washing them in a wave of cool blue. His face is tingling, the light growing. It now covers all of his face, from his hairline to his chin. He can hear what he thinks is a laugh track braying in his mind, voices like scripted dialogue. He shakes it out, and says, "Hey, what do you—"

A clump of dirt hits him in the face. It knocks him flat on his ass. The grave robbing kids take off running.

Jeremy springs forward like a cat in attack mode. He gives chase, quickly gaining on the slowest of the group. The kid, a pudgy little piglet with a mess of blonde hair swooped down in front of his face, tries to zig-zag through the rows of gravestones. But Jeremy knows this cemetery like the back of his hand. He's walked these grounds so many times he can navigate it without even thinking.

The pudgy kid trips over a small stone statue marking the final resting place of someone's beloved curling iron. He sails through the air a few feet and crashes shoulder-first into a gravestone. Dazed, he slumps to the ground and cries out like an injured kitten. The other two grave robbers keep going, thinking: *Better him than us.* Jeremy slows to a trot, stands over the kid. His shirt is ripped and there are twigs and grass in his hair.

"Whoa, dude," the kid says, rubbing his eyes, fighting back tears. "What the hell is wrong with your face?"

"What's wrong with *your* face?" Jeremy counters, out of habit.

The kid rolls his eyes. "No, I mean—"

"You want to tell me what you guys were doing here?" Jeremy cuts in.

The kid looks around nervously, looking for his friends. He scratches his back. Jeremy takes a cautious step back, hand on the nightstick on his belt, thinking the kid might be reaching for a weapon. Management won't let him carry a gun, or even a Taser, says there's no need. He knows it is really because they would have to pay him more if he was licensed to carry a gun.

Jeremy tells the kid to stand up. He leads him back to the security booth at the cemetery's entrance.

As they are walking back the kids says, "Seriously, though, what's up with your face?"

Jeremy almost laughs at the innocence with which the kid asks it. He ignores the question again. He can feel the glow behind his skin getting stronger, knows what will come next. But he can't think of this now. He has work to do. "So," Jeremy says, "do you want to explain it to me now or just wait for the cops?"

The kid tells him to go fuck himself. No longer innocent or naïve. He is facing jail time and needs to act hard. Jeremy calls the cops. Sirens and flashing lights fill the night air in a matter of minutes.

The kid starts to sniffle. Big fat tears build up in his eyes. He's going to burst. Undoing all that hardness in a matter of seconds.

It comes out in a rush, words mixed with sobs, tears, and snot. Lots of snot. "It's just," he says, "just... that there's a lot of money in all of... all of these... these things." He looks unsure of what he is supposed to call the buried appliances, how to explain the grave robbing. "There's a lot... money..." he trails off. The sirens get louder. The sky flashes red and blue, red and blue, like lightning strikes. "My family... We need... money."

13

And with that Jeremy feels bad for the kid. He wishes he could tell him to run, that he'll just tell the cops the grave robbers were too fast for him, gave him the slip. But it's too late. Two cops come jogging into the cemetery. The one time the cops are actually quick about their job and now he has to have a hand in sending some pathetic kid to jail.

The cops take the kid, cuff him immediately, and start shoving him around, asking questions. *What are you doing? Where's the rest of your crew? Where's the loot? How old are you?* Asking each other if they can even legally talk to this punk without his mommy present. The kid just cries.

News vans show up next. Jeremy's not sure how or why. They're all interested in breaking this story. A huge one—grave robbers. They aren't mentioning that it is an appliance cemetery. Probably going to spin it as some teenage voodoo cult. That should crank up the ratings.

Cameras are shoved in Jeremy's face. Questions barked at him. He can hear them in his ears and also in the wires snaking their way through his brain. He can see himself being interviewed in his own head. He closes his eyes, tries to turn off the TV screen in his brain.

The congregation of The Church of TV as God stares at the flickering image of the man with the glowing face on all the TV screens around them. He is everywhere. He is trying to get away from the cameras. They follow him. He hides his face behind his hands.

"There he is," the man in white says. His voice is soft, unsure, almost as if he does not believe what he is seeing. He stares at the screen, committing the image to memory. He feels his heartbeat speed up, knows this is the real thing. The

Great TV in the Sky is showing him this man because he is important. He has to be.

"What'll we do now, Father?" one of the nameless faces calls out to him from the crowd.

But the man in white does not answer. He can't answer because he does not know what they are to do. Not yet.

The man in white leaves the church. He needs to think and pray, and watch TV. His assistant follows him out, but the man in white stops him before they make it out into the warm night. He glares back at his assistant. "Stay," he says. "And for the love of TV, make sure the TiVo is working properly."

"Yes, Father," the assistant says.

He has told his assistant not to call him "Father." It is just too weird. The assistant is his older brother. No older brother should ever call his younger sibling "Father."

The man in white walks into his office in the small building next to the church. The building is also home to a veterinary clinic and an adult bookstore. The man in white's office is a tiny windowless room. The walls are cluttered with posters of long-canceled TV shows, and copies of *TV Guide* from the past twenty years are stacked from floor to ceiling in the corner, partially hiding a small door. The national news report plays on a TV situated on his desk. It shows the man with the glowing face. The TV's speakers do not work, so he is unable to hear what the reporter is reporting. A tagline at the bottom of the screen reads: *Security Guard Stops Attempted Grave Robbing.*

This is interesting, he thinks. He calls for Randall, his assistant, his brother, to come to his office immediately. Randall rushes into the office in a huff. His face is flustered and he appears to be sweating through his gray robe. His nipples are slightly visible through the thin fabric. "Find me this man." The man in white points at the screen. Randall comes around behind the desk to get a look at the man on the TV, like he doesn't know which man he is talking about. "The man with the glowing face," he says. "He's on the news. It shouldn't be too hard—even for you." The words stab at Randall. He might screw things up from time to time, but he is trying. He just wants his brother, the Father, to understand that. And appreciate him for what he does, what he did. Randall left his family to join The Church of TV as God, to follow his brother. He would do anything for the man in white, for The Church of TV as God.

"Find that cemetery," the man in white says, "and then it should be quite easy to find the man." He puts his feet up on his desk, stretches out in his chair. His feet are almost black. No one in The Church of TV as God wears shoes. Or pants. Only loose fitting robes. *The Great TV in the Sky wants you, all of us, to be comfortable, always comfortable,* he tells his followers. *Shoes and pants are evil. They are against all things comfy.*

"Yes, Father," Randall says. His voice skips a beat. He is nervous for the new assignment. He tells himself that he can do it. That he *must* do it. The man in white needs this. The whole church does.

"Damn it, Randall," the man in white says.

"Sorry," Randall says, throwing his hands in the air, slowly backing toward the door. "Sorry," he says, again. "I didn't mean Father. Not Father. No—" And with that he slips out through the door, still walking backwards halfway across the parking lot.

The man in white, relaxes back to watch some TV, his meditation. This is when he feels most comfortable, at peace — sitting in front of the TV, enveloped by that soft blue glow. He feels a part of something, like he is special. He cannot explain it, not really. Words do not do it justice. He has tried, in his teachings in the church, his sermons. His followers say they understand; they feel it too. But they don't, he knows, not like him. The Great TV in the Sky speaks only to him.

This is why he started The Church of TV as God so many years ago. Because, growing up, he felt closer to the TV families he spent afternoons with than his own. His friends at school weren't really his friends. They were fill-ins, space savers, until he could get home and rejoin his real friends.

A few minutes later, while he is lost in the TV bliss, a commercial for dog food or something—it doesn't matter— Randall enters the room, sliding in through a thin crack in the door.

"Sorry to bother you," he says.

The man in white makes a gesture like: *Out with it.*

"We found him."

"You found him?" He throws himself to a standing position, his hands pressed against the desk, as if to hold himself up.

"Yes."

"So soon?"

Randall nods, proud of himself for not screwing this one up. Just so proud.

The man in white asks him how, and Randall says that they just watched the news report again, waited for them to say the name of the cemetery. "We googled it," Randall says, smiles. "Simple, really."

"Brilliant," the man in white says. "This is great news. The Great TV in the Sky is pleased. He will be. I can feel him speaking to me."

Randall smiles at this. He made The Great TV in the Sky happy. "What's next, Father?" he asks.

The man in white is so excited he lets that Father slip. "We have much planning to do, many, many things to

17

work out. We need to go to this man. He needs to hear of his destiny. But first we celebrate."

Randall claps his hands over his head, jumps up and down, giddy. "I'll get the ceremonial wine and your sacred remote."

The man in white nods. "Gather the followers in the church, too, Randall. They shall also hear this splendid news. They shall be involved in this as well."

"Of course," Randall says. He sprints out the door, across the parking lot, and into the dormitory.

It is still dark, but getting light, as Jeremy drives home from work. He is tired, not paying attention. A dog runs out into the street, in front of his car. He slams on his breaks. The dog dives out of the way. There is a tense second when Jeremy thinks he might have hit it, hopes he didn't.

Sitting there, foot on the brake, hands gripping the steering wheel, not breathing. The silence of the early morning is interrupted by a deep, guttural: "Fuck you, man."

Jeremy looks around, searching for the dog's owner, preparing an apology. But it's the dog standing in his window, a little wobbly. Its paws braced against the door frame. "Nice fucking driving. Dude," it says. Jeremy watches the dog. "Didn't you see—" The dog stops, stares at Jeremy for a second, confused.

"I'm sorry," Jeremy says. He's also confused. "But you can ta—"

"Yeah, okay, I can fucking talk and shit. Whoopidee doo. Don't make a big deal of it, okay? And I don't need everyone in the world knowing this shit. My secret, now your secret, too."

Jeremy continues watching the dog, not saying anything.

"Sorry, about that, man," the dog goes on. "Rough day, and all that. You know how it is. Roommates were really riding me about my behavior and shit, so I packed up and moved the hell out of there." The dog offers this with no provocation.

Jeremy nods, says sorry again, and slowly starts to roll away. The dog takes the hint, backs away from the car. Jeremy pulls into his driveway a few houses down, gets out of the car, and the dog is right there, tail wagging. The dog follows him to the front door. "Listen," the dog says, "and you can tell me if this is a little up front or whatever, but considering you almost hit me, I was wondering if you'd mind sparing some food. I'm fucking starving." The dog is a mutt of some kind. Not too big, not too small. Its fur is thick and wiry.

Jeremy shrugs, whatever. He opens the door and the dog runs inside like he owns the place. By the time he gets his shoes off and his coat hung up the dog has already located the bathroom and is drinking greedily from the toilet. "Whoa, there, buddy," Jeremy says, the dog glares at him. "That's gross. I'll get you a bowl of water, just hang on."

"Oh, yay, tap water, gee thanks, mister," the dog says, sarcastically. He follows Jeremy to the kitchen. "My name is Benjamin."

"Excuse me?"

"You called me buddy, but that's not my name. My name is Benjamin."

Jeremy smiles, nods.

"And I don't like to be called Benny or Benji, or any other gay ass shit like that. Pup, Puppy, none of that fuck all." He is very serious about this. "It's Benjamin."

19

"Got it," Jeremy says, looks for something to give the dog to eat. He doesn't have dog food in the house so he feeds Benjamin bologna. The dog grumbles about it for a second but gives up quickly, gulps the lunch meat down in a few bites.

After he is done eating, Jeremy asks him, "Roommates?"

The dog nods. "Yeah, they sucked, always trying to get me to do things. Sit. Speak. Roll over. Little tricks. 'Stop licking yourself there, Benny.' Well, how the hell else am I supposed to clean it, huh?"

"By roommates, though, you mean owners, right?"

"The fuck you just say to me?" Benjamin growls, thick white spittle builds in the corners of his mouth. "Nobody fucking owns me, you hear me? I'm my own man."

"But you're a dog."

"Oh, really? I'm a dog?" Benjamin starts sniffing about the kitchen, moves to the living room. "That's all I am, huh?" He lifts his leg next to the sofa, glares back at Jeremy. "Sorry mister," the dog says. "I didn't mean to piss all over your couch, honest. But... I just don't know any better. I'm just a poor little doggie."

"Okay, I'm sorry," Jeremy says. "Please, just don't do that. I didn't realize it was such a sensitive subject."

"Well, it fucking is. You'd better realize it pretty quick or living together is going to get very complicated, very fast."

"Whoa," Jeremy says, "living together? I just—"

Benjamin looks at him, lifts his leg again, like he's saying: *I don't want to do this, but I will if I have to.*

Jeremy shrugs, thinks: *It might be nice to have a dog, a friend.* He's never had a dog, always wanted one growing up, and he is pretty lonely, as it is.

Benjamin lowers his leg, wags his tail. "We're going to be the best of friends," he says. "You'll see. You're going to love having me around."

"So, let me ask you something," Benjamin says. "What the hell is wrong with your face? No offense or anything."

Jeremy is starting to get used to this question. It's been coming up more and more lately, with his more recent transformations. He takes a deep breath, tells the dog that he is turning into a TV. He is sad and tells the story with compassion and humility. Benjamin bursts out laughing, rolling on the ground, tongue slapping around. "That's the stupidest shit I've ever heard. A TV? You're seriously turning into a fucking TV?"

Jeremy nods.

"How is that even possible? I've never heard of anyone turning into a TV, and my roommates used to leave all those daytime talk shows on for me when they were gone, so I wouldn't feel like I was alone all day. You know those shows that have all the freak-o people on them? Fat chicks that are actually guys but still want their straight boyfriends to accept them. Sixteen year old sluts that don't know who their baby-daddy is, because they've fucked so many dudes. People who are into horses. Shit like that."

"Okay, just stop, I know the shows you're talking about."

"Yeah, well, I've never seen anyone on those shows turning into a TV. Hey, I've got a great idea..."

"No," Jeremy says, "I'm not going on one of those shows. They're not real anyway. It's all made up."

"You're kidding me?"

Jeremy shakes his head, No, it's true.

"So, a fucking TV, huh? What, like, happens to all your... uh, inside stuff when you become a TV?"

Jeremy doesn't know.

"I mean, do you, like, die? Can a person live as a TV?"

21

Jeremy shrugs again. These are all things he's been wondering himself, things he's been worrying about. His father bailed before his own transformation was complete, and Jeremy has no idea what happened to him, in the end.

"That's fucked up, man."

The man in white tells his church that The Great TV in the Sky has shown him their savior. He tells them that their time has come. He tells them that tomorrow he, along with a few other chosen followers, will venture out to bring this man back to them, the man with the glowing face. But, he tells them, not to worry about this now, for now they celebrate. He blesses the ceremonial wine in the name of the TV, the remote, and the Holy outlet. And they party.

The man in white wakes up next to Margaret. His head pounds from too much wine. He is naked, and so is Margaret. He rolls out of bed, trying to be quiet, to not wake her. He wonders how he could have let this happen. Out of all of his followers, how did he end up with Margaret? *She's old*, he thinks, *but so am I*. She's older, he tells himself.

Margaret is already awake. She is watching him, had been watching him sleep. "Good morning, Father," she says.

Her voice startles him. "Ah, Margaret, yes, uh... good morning." He crawls out of the bed and looks around the room for his robe, can't find it anywhere. "Yes." He inches toward the door, covering himself with his hands. "Today is going to be a great day."

"Yeah," she says, sitting up, moving forward, eager for him to stay. "I'm very excited about what is happening." She wraps the blanket around her body. She is flabby in parts that should not be flabby. The man in white flinches.

22

Margaret moves closer to him. "How do you think The Great TV in the Sky will present himself to us, Father?" she says.

"That has not been revealed to me yet," he says, going into preacher-mode, anything to take his mind off what has happened here, anything to change the subject. "With time, my dear." He touches her face, immediately regrets it. "The Great TV in the Sky answers all questions, with time. He will tell us when He feels we are worthy."

She swoons at his words, at his touch. He can see the love in her eyes. It is too much. "I am excited and nervous and anxious," she says, thinks: *and horny*. She touches herself under the blankets.

"Do not be, my child." He has to separate himself from her, let her know that he is her spiritual leader, not her lover. "Do not trouble yourself with such thoughts. Everything is already in motion. Things will happen when they are meant to. We cannot worry too much about minor details. All we can do is trust that The Great TV in the Sky knows what He is doing, and that we are a part of Him, and He a part of us."

Margaret smiles at this.

"Now, my child, I have one question for you," the man in white says. "Have you seen my robe?"

Margaret glances around at the floor, making a big show of it. "No, sorry, Father, I have not."

The man in white goes to the door, leaves the room. Margaret falls onto the bed. She has the man in white's robe stuffed under her pillow.

The Church of TV as God is a mess. There are plastic cups and papers scattered everywhere. They must have really partied hard in celebration of the things to come. People, church members, are passed out here and there in the church, draped across TV seats, in the aisles, too drunk to have made it to their own beds in the dormitory.

The man in white is slightly embarrassed by this. He should have had more control than this, of himself and his followers. He should not have given in to temptations of the flesh so easily. What will The Great TV in the Sky think of their behavior here? He crosses the sanctuary to the flat screen TV altar. Kneels before it, blesses himself with the sign of the TV—a square around his heart. He is dressed in a new, clean robe. He prays to The Great TV in the Sky, begs for forgiveness, asks for guidance on how to proceed.

Randall is outside, packing up the church's minivan for their trip. The others set to join them are helping load the van. The man in white says one final pray and goes about getting himself ready. He makes a mental note to set the TiVo to record all the shows he will miss while they are out on the road.

Jeremy's head feels heavier when he wakes up. His temples have started turning into wood. His head is boxier.

He is surprised that it does not hurt, turning into a TV. By the way his father reacted during his own slow transformation, Jeremy was expecting it to be painful. It is actually quite pleasant. His head is full of TV static, floating around, fluttering about like a snowstorm. A breezy feeling.

He can hear Benjamin running around downstairs, back and forth, from one end of the house to the other. Benjamin is saying things but Jeremy cannot make the words out.

When he gets downstairs, he sees Benjamin doing what he can only describe as the pee-pee dance.

"Why are all these fucking doors locked, man?" Benjamin hiss-growls. "I'm about to explode over here."

"Want to go for a walk?" Jeremy asks.

Benjamin wags his tail and does a little dance at the door. "You're a dick," he says, when Jeremy laughs at him. "I just like walks is all. I can't help it. Just even hearing the word 'walk' gets me all fucking amped up." His tail wags harder and faster.

"Most dogs do."

Outside, Benjamin moves quickly from tree to tree to mailbox to flower pot, peeing on just about everything, things he likes or hates, Jeremy does not know which it is, does not understand the nuances of how or why dogs mark things.

"Are you supposed to be on a leash or something?" Jeremy asks. "Isn't that some new law—all dogs must be leashed?"

"Naw, I'm cool," Benjamin says. He moves over to a new tree and stares up into a tangle of branches. A squirrel moves about up there, doing squirrel things. This, based on instinct alone, pisses Benjamin off. He tries to climb the tree, but dogs are not very good at climbing trees, and he only manages to scamper up a foot or two before sliding back down to the ground. The squirrel doesn't even acknowledge him. "Asshole," Benjamin growls up the tree, "you're lucky... this time," and moves along, glancing back at the squirrel a few final times.

"So, I was wondering," Jeremy says, as they continue walking.

"Oh, this should be good," the dog sighs. "Go on."

"Are there a lot of you..."

"You mean dogs? Uh, yeah there are quite a few of us in the world."

"Not just dogs. I mean talking dogs?"

"I don't fucking know, man. It's not like we have weekly meetings and shit." He huffs, shakes his head.

"Oh," is all Jeremy can say.

"You ask a lot of stupid questions, do you know that? The youngest of my former roommates asked a lot of questions, like you. I think he might have been retarded, or challenged, or slow, or what the fuck ever you people call it these days. In my world we just call it dead, because you won't last long with a faulty brain. Anyway, you kind of remind me of him, the kid. Are you retarded? That would explain a lot." Benjamin laughs at this, at his own question. He stops to pee on a small garden gnome, saying, "Help, help me, I'm drowning," in a small squeaky, gnomey voice.

Jeremy ignores him, doesn't want to argue, especially not in public.

A white minivan turns the corner and drives past them so slow it is practically standing still. The van is full of people with shaved heads. Seven people, all who are identical except for the driver. He has long white hair. All seven of them stare at Jeremy and Benjamin as they pass, looking back over their shoulders when they are too far down the road. One of them waves.

"What was that about?" Benjamin asks, sniffing the gnome and moving along.

"Is that him?" Randall asks from the passenger seat as the van turns the corner. He is pointing at a man walking a dog further up the street.

"Possibly," the man in white says, and the six other passengers bless themselves with the sign of the TV, making a square around their hearts.

"I think it is. I bet it is," Randall says. "It probably is. Right?"

They drive closer, to get a better look. They are going slow. "Look at the face. It glows. That is him, is it not?" asks one of the other followers from the backseat. The man in

26

white hates the way in which some of his followers speak. It's like some weird cult gibberish, all holier than thou and really creepy. He feels it makes a mockery of his church, his faith.

They are right next to the man and his dog now. They all turn in their seats to watch him as they pass.

"Yes," another one in back says, "that is him. That face. It is the one from the TV news report. It is." He passes up a sheet of folded paper. It is a printout of a close up of the man's face.

That is him, the man in white thinks. The savior is standing right there, not twenty feet away. He can feel him. He can feel the man's power and will in his heart.

"Shall we go?" Randall asks, making a move like he is going to open the door.

The man in white grabs him by the robe, holds him in place. "No," he says. "Not yet." There is much grumbling from the others in the car. "We are not yet ready for that," the man in white says. "The Great TV in the Sky will tell us when the time has come." The man in white continues driving, past the man with the glowing face, their savior. They all turn in their seats to watch him. Randall waves at him. The others bless themselves with the sign of the TV again.

At work, Jeremy hears soft chanting coming from the TV section of the appliance cemetery. He does not come into this part of the cemetery often. It freaks him out, reminds him of what he is becoming. He wonders if, when he dies, he will be buried in an appliance cemetery or a normal, people cemetery. He wonders where his father is buried. He wonders a lot of things, but they are interrupted by Benjamin.

"Well, what the hell are you waiting for?" he says. Benjamin had insisted on coming to work with Jeremy. He said he had to see what an appliance cemetery was. The first thing he said about it was that it was fucking stupid, and so were people for burying their appliances. Jeremy explained to him that not all people buried their appliances, and Benjamin said that he still thought people were stupid. He's spent the rest of his time at work with Jeremy complaining, licking his own crotch, and falling asleep on his back, legs moving like he was chasing squirrels in a dream. The chanting woke him up.

Jeremy snaps out of his daze and takes the first step into TV Land, as some of the other guards have taken to calling it.

TV Land is the largest part of the cemetery. There are more TVs buried in the appliance cemetery than every other kind of appliance combined. This is maybe because newer TVs are not made to last longer than five or ten years. And it is almost more expensive to get them fixed when they do break down than it is to just buy a new one.

The chanting gets louder the deeper into TV Land they go. It is dark, and Jeremy's face is glowing brighter than it ever has before. Benjamin says, "Man, I don't know if I'll ever get used to that. It's some freaky ass shit."

"I've gotten used to the fact that I've spent the last few days talking almost exclusively to a dog."

"Oh, yeah, I've been meaning to bring that up. What's up with that? You're kind of a pathetic man-child, aren't you? Don't you have any friends? A special lady in your life? I bet you haven't been laid in years."

"Ouch," Jeremy says without much sincerity. Benjamin's insults do not even faze him anymore.

"No offense," Benjamin says. "I just mean that—"

"*Sssssssssh*," Jeremy hisses.

Benjamin mumbles, "Well, fuck you, too," under his breath.

"Look." Jeremy points at four men standing around a grave. He doesn't approach. They fall back and watch the men, squatting low behind a gravestone.

"Are these more of those grave robbers you busted?"

"I don't think so." Jeremy crawls forward on hands and knees. Benjamin wonders if he looks this stupid from behind when he walks. He decides that, no, he doesn't. He probably looks all kinds of badass from behind.

"They look like they are… praying," Jeremy says.

The four men stand in a small semi-circle around a gravestone, holding hands. They are all dressed the same—gray robes, shaved heads, thin white chin-strap beards.

"Oh, no shit," Benjamin says, too loud. "It's a goddamn cult."

The four men stop chanting, stop praying, but they do not move. They stand there holding hands and staring down at the grave, at the grass.

Jeremy's face tingles. The static behind his eyes intensifies. He glows brighter.

The four men turn toward him. A fifth man steps out from behind some trees in the distance. He wears an elaborate white robe and has a full head of bright white hair, which seems to glow. He can't be a day over forty, too young to be so completely white. He steps up to the four others. They bow their heads to him.

"That must be the cult leader," Benjamin says out of the corner of his mouth.

"Will you shut up?"

The man continues walking. He is heading toward Jeremy and Benjamin. Jeremy looks around, nervous, thinks about running. But he is too curious to do anything other

29

than stand and watch. Benjamin is more cautious. The fur on his back stands straight up. He arches his back like he is trying to make himself look bigger, tougher. A quick flash of fangs, that usually does the job. But the man keeps walking. Benjamin gives up on trying to look tough. His tail disappears between his legs. Now he makes himself look small, non-threatening. When the man is about five feet away, Benjamin says, "Oh, fuck this—I'm fucking out of here," and runs off back the way they came, whimpering.

The man stops in front of Jeremy. He smells a bit like BO and his hair is not glowing as much as it appeared from far away. He reaches a hand out, touches Jeremy's cheek, real soft. His skin is clammy. He closes his eyes as the glow from Jeremy's face washes over him, taking it all in. Jeremy shoves the man's hand away.

"Do you know who I am?" the man asks, eyes still closed. "Do you know why I have come here?"

Jeremy takes a step back. "No," he says.

"I have come here to deliver a message to you," the man says. "A message from God."

"Okay, whatever," Jeremy says, not really caring what this man has to say. "But listen, the cemetery's closed for the night. I'm not even sure how you got in here, the gate is locked. But you and your friends will have to come back to worship... or whatever tomorrow, when we are open." Jeremy looks over at the other men, they are still holding hands, and have begun pray-chanting again.

"I run a small church," he says, not listening. Maybe you've heard of it—The Church of TV as God?"

Jeremy shakes his head, no. He wonders, *what the hell kind of church is that*? "TV?" he says. "As in television?"

The man in white ignores the question. "I know what you are," he says, "what you are becoming." He reaches out and touches Jeremy's cheeks again. His eyes shoot open, perfectly white now, pupils almost gone—pinpoint. His blue irises are almost gray. They glow. Jeremy feels this in the static in his mind, a change in frequency.

The man in white puts his hands up, like he is surrendering. He makes a simple motion, a small inconspicuous gesture, and two more men dressed in gray robes come at Jeremy from the sides. They wrap their arms around him. They pin him to the ground, his face buried in grass, damp blades tickling his nostrils. He feels a knee press into his spine, his arms tied behind his back.

Jeremy is pulled to a standing position. The man in white is already walking away. The other four men in gray robes come toward him now.

"What the fuck?" Benjamin howls, trying to cover his words with barks. It does not work. "What the fuck are you doing?"

One of the men throws a heavy black bag over Jeremy's head. The inside smells of vomit. He can hear Benjamin screaming, a mix of words and growls.

"Quiet that mutt," someone says. There is the sound of a struggle and Benjamin yips out in pain.

Jeremy tries to tell them to stop, but when he opens his mouth nothing comes out. He feels something big and heavy slam into his chest. The breath in his lungs rushes out like a popped balloon. He hits the ground and everything goes so black it's like he never existed at all.

Jeremy wakes to the sound of a constant thum-thruming, as well as Benjamin whimpering. The bag is still on his head, but he can tell they are in a car, the van, driving fast. Probably on a highway. Benjamin's shaking body is pressed tightly against his own. He catches a quick glimpse of the dog through a gap in the bottom of the bag over his head. He is a mess. Fur matted with blood, his legs are shaking, his whole body twitches. He is scared, and so is Jeremy. Jeremy does not understand what is going on, why this is happening. Other than this, everything is silent and black and empty. The people in the car are not speaking. There is no music playing. No anything. He blacks out again.

Part Two: The Great TV in the Sky

Jeremy hears a familiar voice. The world around him is still dark, but he is no longer crammed into the back of the van. He is able to stretch out a bit. But not much. His arms are still bound behind his back.

"These ties are not necessary," the familiar voice says. "He will no longer be any trouble. Will you, my son?"

Jeremy mumbles something like *Fuck you* but shakes his head no. He will not be any more trouble.

The ropes are cut from his wrists, and his arms drop to his sides, hanging numb, lifeless. The bag is pulled off and light attacks his eyes. The world comes into slow focus and the man in white, smiling, appears before him. His eyes are watering. He makes the sign of the TV around his heart and takes a seat in front of Jeremy.

They are sitting in a room made of TVs. Hundreds of TVs all set to different channels. Jeremy looks around at all the screens, all the different images. The walls seem to move, pulse with life.

"Welcome to my church," the man in white says. Jeremy can hear people milling around, through the door at the back of the church. "You have changed again. Would you like to see this new level of your transformation?" He holds up a small hand mirror before Jeremy has a chance to answer.

Jeremy's head is now perfectly square. His face is still his own, still human. But it is framed by dark, polished

33

wood. His antennas have also grown, they now stick up six inches over the top of his head.

He continues to stare at his reflection in the mirror. He is becoming an older model TV, one with big metal knobs for changing the channel and the volume, same as his father was turning into, before he left. Big and heavy. He touches his face. There is almost no feeling left in it, no sensation of skin on skin.

"It is beautiful," the man in white tells him.

Jeremy knocks the mirror out of his hand. It shatters on the ground. The man in white never takes his eyes off of him.

"What am I doing here?" Jeremy asks. "Why did you bring me here? Where... where is my dog?"

"Slow down, my son, breathe. One question at a time. I told you when we met that I would answer all of your questions. Your dog, Benjamin, is fine. We had to tie him out back. He is a feisty little thing, no? He bit a few of my people. Should we be worried about this? Are his shots up-to-date?"

Jeremy shrugs and the man in white lets it go. "You can see him later. First, I would like to show you something. Come with me."

The man in white leads Jeremy out of the church. In the hallway a crowd has gathered. They all try to get in close enough to catch a glimpse of the man said to be their savior, the man with the TV head. They whisper to each other as Jeremy passes them. They smile and bow their heads out of respect. Some of them cry. Girls discuss how cute they think he is, how they would totally bang him given the chance. They giggle and hide behind their hands when he looks at them. A middle-aged woman holds her baby out in front of Jeremy. Jeremy looks at the baby, unsure of what she is doing, and nods. It looks like a fine baby, he guesses. He thinks about touching the baby, but doesn't. The woman looks confused, too, and the man in white nods at her. She slips back into the crowd, only to be instantly replaced with someone else just as eager to get close to Jeremy, to be blessed by him, saved. To see him.

As they push their way further through the crowd, Jeremy thinks: *What the hell is going on here? Who are all these people? Why are they all dressed like this? Maybe Benjamin was right, maybe this is a cult.*

They make it through the crowd, out the doors, and into the ever-darkening night. Jeremy has no idea where he is. They are in some city, but he does not recognize anything around him. It looks generic, like just about every other city across the country. Nothing stands out, no landmarks. No Sears Tower or Statue of Liberty or Space Needle to give it away. Jeremy can hear Benjamin barking, bark-swearing, from somewhere in the distance.

They enter a small building next to the church, follow the narrow hallways to the man in white's cramped office. The man in white begins to explain things to Jeremy. He tells him about the church, what they do. He tells Jeremy about the prophecy he received from The Great TV in the Sky, how a man—half man, half TV—will present himself to the church. How this TV man will help bring about the second coming of The Great TV in the Sky. How he knows Jeremy is this man. That he is the one The Great TV in the Sky spoke of.

Jeremy does not believe any of what he is told.

The man in white stares at him, at his glowing face. "How can I prove this to you?" he wonders out loud. "Follow me. I would like to show you something else." He stands up and moves over to the small door at the back of the office. He steps into the darkness of the room, fumbles around on the wall for the light switch. He finds it, flips it on. Jeremy steps inside. It is cramped and claustrophobic.

The man in white steps up to a table in the middle of the room. There is a body on the table. "If all I have told you is not true, how do you explain this?" It is the body of a young woman. She is naked, a sheet covering her from the waist down. She has a TV head. "I have created this—her," the man in white says, "at the direction of The Great TV in the Sky. He has given me the power to create this life when there was not one there to begin with. This is the second part of the prophecy. This woman, she is to be your wife. The Eve to your Adam, if you will."

"Is she—" Jeremy starts.

"Alive? Yes. She is very much alive. I have told you—I was given the power to give her life. I created her."

"You created her?"

"Yes, in a sense. She is a human that I turned into a TV. Her brain was long dead before I found her, and I saved her. Repurposed her, if you like that analogy better. She was a broken machine that I made work again. That I made better."

"How—"

"Do not worry about the specifics, my son. The Great TV in the Sky has shown me how. Just know that you are to be married to her, posthaste. Once she is ready we will bring the two of you together, as man and wife. You will mate. You will create a perfect TV baby. This baby will be the second coming of The Great TV in the Sky." He blesses himself with the sign of the TV, blesses the TV woman on the table.

The body on the table moves. Just a finger, a small twitch. The man in white smiles, looks back at Jeremy. "See," he says to him, "she is alive." He turns his attention to the TV woman. "Lay still, my child, you are not yet strong enough to move. Soon. Be patient."

Jeremy notices all of the wires connecting her to a row of ancient-looking machines. The wires disappear behind her TV head, plugged into whatever is left of her brain. The man in white adjusts some dials on the machines. Her TV screen flickers to life. It shows the close up image of a beautiful woman's face. She stares out though the screen, eyes jumping all around the room.

Jeremy stands over her. She looks into his eyes, deep. She is terrified, he can tell, unsure of what is happening to her. "Is she in pain?" he asks the man in white.

"At the moment I do not know whether or not she can feel anything."

"She looks like she is in pain."

"Her body is trying to reject the transplant."

"You mean the TV?"

"Yes, the TV," the man in white. "I have fused her brain with the inner workings of the TV. Once they grow together, accept each other, she will be complete. She will be perfect."

Jeremy wakes in a small room that is more like a prison cell than a bedroom. The door is heavy wood and triple locked. His bed is nothing more than a cot with a blanket thrown across it. The walls are padded. There are no windows.

He hears footsteps echoing through the hallway, approaching his door. A key jingles in the locks, one after the other, until the door slides open a crack. A young girl slips inside and the door closes behind her. She is only about seven or eight, if that, Jeremy guesses. She holds a tray of food out for him to take. He stares at the tray for a second, sees her little arms shaking under the strain of holding it out.

"Thank you." He takes the tray from her and sets it down on the bed next to him.

The girl bows slightly. She turns to leave. She looks sickly, like a cancer patient, with her shaved head and pale skin.

"Wait," Jeremy says. She stops, but does not turn to face him. "Can I ask you a question?"

She looks at him now, says nothing. She taps her bare foot against the ground, like this is all taking too long.

"What is your name?"

"Lucy," she answers.

Jeremy tells her his name. She does not seem to know who he is, who he is supposed to be. Like she has never heard of him. Is only here now because she is following orders.

"Lucy," he says, "have you seen my dog?" Jeremy is surprised at how worried he is about the dog. The furry little asshole has grown on him since he invited himself to live in Jeremy's house. He is the only living thing Jeremy knows in this place, the only one he has any kind of connection with.

The girl nods. She drags her bare foot back and forth across the floor, staring down at it, not making eye contact.

"Is he okay?"

Lucy nods again. "He is fine," she says. "He is very cute. I like him a lot." She blushes, and Jeremy sees her for the child she is. "I have not seen a puppy for a very long time," she says. "I used to have one of my own, before we came to live here. We are not allowed to have pets here."

It is now Jeremy's turn to nod. He doesn't know what to say.

"Your puppy is very funny. And he talks! He tells funny jokes, with lots of curse words."

"Can you do me a favor, please? Can you tell my dog—his name is Benjamin—that I am safe and that everything will be okay, and that I will see him soon?"

Lucy laughs at this. "Benjamin is not a doggie name. It's a people name."

Jeremy shrug-smiles at this. "Will you tell him?"

Lucy nods and slips back out into the hallway. Jeremy passes the rest of the day pacing back and forth across the room, bouncing off the padded walls.

A different girl brings him dinner. She is just as young as Lucy and she will not make eye contact with him. He does not eat the food. Just like he did not eat the breakfast Lucy brought him. And just like he will not eat the next meal either. He does not trust these people. He will not eat food prepared by them.

The man in white watches as Jeremy paces his room on a camera hidden in the corner. He has been watching Jeremy do this since he arrived at the church. He has been pacing for three days. He is like an unhappy zoo animal, yearning for the world beyond his cage. Trays of untouched food are building up in the corner. He has not eaten a single scrap of food. The man in white is beginning to worry about him. This is not healthy. He cannot help usher in the second coming of The Great TV in the Sky if he dies from starvation.

The man in white calls Randall into the office. "Check on the girl, please," he says. He leans back in his chair and shuts his eyes, feet up on the desk. The chair squeaks as he rocks himself like a baby in a cradle. The members of the church are starting to ask questions, wondering about the man sent to them by The Great TV in the Sky. He is running out of things to tell them.

None of them even know about the TV woman. Randall is the only other person in the church to know about her. Randall walks into the back room, calls for the man in white before he even gets all the way in.

She is awake, sitting up on the table. Her long legs dangle a few inches above the floor. Her TV screen face is lit up, showing no more pain. She now displays a look of mild confusion. She looks about the room, unsure of where she is, who she is.

"Hello," the man in white says, stepping closer to her. She backs away from him, afraid of him. "Don't worry, my child," he says, taking on his comforting, preacher voice. "You are safe now. Do not be afraid. I am here to help you."

She relaxes a bit, his voice comforts her. It is familiar.

"Tell me the last thing you remember, my child," the man in white says.

The TV woman tries to think back, to remember. There is much darkness in her memory, many missing chunks. She starts to get scared, worried about all of the holes in her memory. "N-nothing," she says, finally, her voice coming through the TV's speakers. "I can't remember." She starts to cry, her image flickering in and out of focus on the screen.

"Please," the man in white says. He touches her arm and her face reappears on the screen. "Please do not cry. Everything will become clear to you soon. You will see."

She stops crying, just like that.

"Now tell me, do you know what your name is?"

She thinks about it for a few seconds. "Eve?" she says, more a question than a statement.

The man in white nods, thinking that it is as good as any other name. She must have heard him telling Jeremy that they are to be like the Adam and Eve of The Church of TV as God. He is not aware of what her true name is, does not wish to scare her more by telling her it is not Eve.

The man in white turns to Randall, who is staring off into space like he is dreadfully bored with all of this, like he would rather be doing something, anything else, than helping to bring about the second coming of The Great TV in the Sky. "Get me the boy," he says. He also hands Randall a duffle bag and tells him to have Jeremy wear what's inside.

Randall salutes him and rushes off, stumbling over his big, bare feet.

The man in white turns back to Eve, the TV girl. She is staring at her fingers, wiggling them, amazed by what they are capable of. She slides off the table, her feet gently connecting with the cold tile floor. She stands, wobbles. "Take it easy, my child. You need to go slow, please. You may not be ready for all of this, and we don't want to hurt ourselves, do we?" He helps her sit back down. She smiles up at him, although she is not sure why. She feels comfortable with him.

Jeremy stares at the eve-growing pile of untouched food in the corner of his room. He is starving. The food mocks him. His stomach begs him to eat some, just a bite, anything. But he can't. The food is poisoned, he is sure.

Out of the corner of his eyes, he spots a fly circling the food. Some of it is rotten, most of it, and the fly buzzes around crazily.

With reflexes he doesn't even know he possesses, he throws his hand out, catches the fly in the air. He stuffs it into his mouth. It buzzes around in there for a second before he bites down on it. Its blood spurts in his mouth, slightly sour. It is not enough. It leaves him unsatisfied, still hungry. He licks his lips, trying to get every last bit of the fly.

The door swings open and he jumps back onto the bed, frightened.

Randall steps into the room. Jeremy recognizes him from the cemetery, praying around the grave of some

41

forgotten TV. Randall is carrying a small duffle bag now. "Put this on," he tosses the bag onto the bed, "and come with me."

Jeremy ignores the duffle bag. "Where are we going?" he asks.

"Put the clothes on and come with me," Randall repeats.

Jeremy gives up. He knows if he asks any other questions he will just get the same response. He reluctantly unzips the bag. There is a faded black suit stuffed in it, not folded, crumpled into a ball. He looks up at Randall, asks for some privacy, maybe. Randall does not respond. He steps out into the hall, waiting for Jeremy to get changed. He crosses his arms in front of his body, holding his right wrist in his left hand. Many years ago, before the church, before The Great TV in the Sky, he was a prison guard. He spent a lot of time standing like this. He still likes to do it sometimes, for sentimental reasons. It is how he meditates. How he channels The Great TV in the Sky. Everyone does it in their own way.

The suit does not fit at all. The pants are too tight and too short. The shirt and the jacket must be made for a child. Jeremy can barely button half of the buttons. He goes barefoot since his shoes were taken when he first arrived, and there aren't any in the duffle bag.

Walking through the halls, Jeremy realizes this is some kind of dormitory. Most of the rooms they pass, the ones with open doors, look like comfortable little studio apartments—beds, TVs, microwaves, mini-fridges. Just like college. Not like his. His room has been converted into a prison cell.

"Where are we going?" he tries again, now that he has put on the suit and they are on the move.

"Back to the church."

"Can I ask you about this church?" Jeremy says. Randall just looks at him, which he takes as an okay to ask. "What's up with this place? I mean the robes and the shaved heads? All the TVs? What kind of church does all that?" Randall still does not say anything. "And I take it from all these rooms that you all live here." He's trying not to say the "C" word, assuming people in cults don't like to call what they're doing that. That's why they call this place a church. It's not The Cult of TV as God.

Jeremy thinks that most churches are basically cults. This one just took it a step further.

Randall just walks.

The church is packed. All of the TV seats have people sitting in them. The congregation is quiet, sitting patiently. They all look forward, at the large TV screen hanging above the altar. It only shows static. They are mesmerized by it, seem to be praying to it. Their lips move in silent words. Randall and Jeremy enter the church from a side door, so as not to disturb the praying congregation.

The man in white meets them behind the sanctuary, out of sight of the congregation. He is wearing a new clean white robe, this one nicer than his last. It is more ceremonial, a white stole draped across his shoulders. His long white hair is combed back, off his face. "Very nice," he says, inspecting Jeremy. "It is a little small, but it should work fine." He straightens Jeremy's collar. "Do not worry, my son, you will only be wearing these clothes for a short time. And then you can take them off."

The man in white tells Randall to get the girl. He turns back to Jeremy. "Wait here," he says. He then walks out onto the sanctuary, paces in front of the altar, the large screen still full of TV static behind him. He talks to his congregation for a minute, blessing them in the name of The Great TV in the Sky.

43

He says, "I have called you all here tonight, not just to pray and be in the presence of The Great TV in the Sky's loving embrace, but to also share something very important with you. Tonight, our prophecies will come true. Tonight will bring about the second coming of The Great TV in the Sky. It has been said to me, both in my teachings and in my private prayers, that The Great TV in the Sky will come to us as a child. A child of great power and heavenly grace. This child will show us the way to salvation. He will come to us and lead us back to the Land of TVs. He will take us home."

The congregation talks amongst themselves for a minute, voices coming over like a wave. All anxious for what will happen next.

The man in white raises his hands to gather his congregation's attention again. "Tonight," he says, "we celebrate a marriage."

He goes on to explain Jeremy and Eve, and how it is from them that The Great TV in the Sky will be reborn. Jeremy peeks out at the church, at the sea of shaved heads, gray robes. All the talking and chattering building up again, growing louder.

Randall steps up next to Jeremy. The girl with the TV head, Eve, stands behind him. She is wearing a white dress, a wedding dress. She glances at Jeremy, the face on her TV screen blushes. She knows who he is, that they are to be married. The man in white comes back to meet them. The two of them, Jeremy and Eve, are ushered out in front of the church. They are stripped naked. Jeremy quickly covers himself with his hands. Eve, knowing nothing of shame for her humanly body, does not. She stands completely at ease. They are walked down the aisle, past every member of The Church of TV as God. The church members stare in awe at the TV people, the heavenly couple. They bless them with the sign of the TV, pray for them. After the parading of their naked bodies, they are lead out the back of the church.

There are no wedding ceremonies in The Church of TV as God. Just the couple to be married and The Great TV in the Sky alone in a room together. The only three that matter for this short time. They must promise themselves to each other and then consummate the marriage under the gaze of TV static, said to be The Great TV in the Sky projected into the room with them. During the process, the rest of the church gathers together and prays for the newlyweds. They are all connected in this way. If the couple is to be accepted by The Great TV in the Sky, the woman will have become pregnant after their first time together. If the woman does not become pregnant, the couple's marriage is deemed a failure and they will be forced to divorce. Marriage is just a means for procreation. For the betterment of the church and all of its members.

The man in white leads Jeremy and Eve through the church, to the marriage room. He explains the process to them on the walk over. They are still naked. Eve has been staring at Jeremy the entire time. She is not listening to the man in white. She knows all of what he is saying, has been programmed for it. She has been made to believe in it. She finds that, although she has just met this man and has never shared a single word with him, she is very much attracted to him. This is also probably just part of her programming, too, she thinks. But maybe not. She knows that they will have a baby together. It is their destiny. She also knows that this baby is going to save all of the people here.

The man in white leaves them in the room. He stands outside the door for a few moments, hoping things go according to plan. He blesses the door with the sign of the TV, and then he leaves them to it.

A TV screen takes up an entire wall in the marriage room. It is already showing the TV static of The Great TV in the Sky. He is in the room waiting for them. Waiting for them to swear themselves to each other and to Him. Waiting to be reborn. Eve can feel it, a buzzing in all her circuitry. The Great TV in the Sky is very powerful.

Jeremy paces the room, nervous. Eve sits on the bed, waits for him to come to her. She watches him, her TV eyes never leaving his body. She is beautiful in the cool darkness of the TV static. Jeremy looks at her, really looks at her for the first time, sees her beauty. His antennas buzz slightly, a tingle, causing his heart to beat a little faster. He feels lightheaded. "Come to me," Eve finally says, tired of waiting, hungry to taste him, to make him her husband.

This is the first time Jeremy has heard her speak. Her voice, coming through the small speakers at the base of her TV head, is young, innocent. He sits next to her, still covering himself with cupped hands.

"What is your name?" she asks. Her words almost out of sync with the movement of her lips.

"Jeremy."

"Jeremy." She tries it out, feeling it on her lips and tongue, seems confused by it. "Jeremy," she repeats, thinks about it. "I like it. It is beautiful… just like you." She blushes now. Her face flickers on her screen.

Jeremy stares at her face; it is just the projection of an image of a face. He tries to imagine it as real, as flesh. He reaches out to touch it. It is just glass, smooth, featureless. The glass is warm against his fingers. She looks up at him with her fake eyes, touches his face in the same way. She is shocked by the texture of his skin. "It is not like mine," she says, touches her own face, raps her knuckles against the glass.

"No, not yet at least."

"I do not understand what you mean by this." She places her hands inside his. She is ready to promise herself to him, for now and forever. She is ready to consummate their marriage in the presence of The Great TV in the Sky.

He tries to think of the simplest way possible to explain this to her, comes up blank. He opens his mouth, and she leans forward to kiss him. She presses her glass lips against his mouth. Something passes between them. Sparks, maybe, or love. Or just a static zap from the electricity behind her screen. She leans back, smiling, a smear of his lips printed over her own. She kisses him again, harder.

Eve moans softly, her speakers crackle. The wooden frames of their TV heads clunk together. There is no feeling to it. After a minute, Jeremy lets himself get lost in the kiss. They are both moaning now, groping each other. Eve pushes him over on top of the bed, climbs on top of him. He is inside of her before he is even aware of it. Her insides pulse with electricity. Static washes over him. She stops kissing him, pulls back to look into his eyes.

"Are we married?" she asks.

Jeremy shrugs.

She kisses him again. "I believe we are."

Jeremy looks over at the TV static playing on the wall, thinking how weird it is. The thought brings a small smile to his face. He hadn't been prepared for this; it happened so fast. Even though he hasn't spoken to her in years, he wonders what his mother will think. Maybe this is what he is supposed to do with his life. Maybe, like the man in white said, this is his destiny.

"Will you make me pregnant now?" she asks him. She parts her lips in a dreamy smile.

The question throws him off a bit. He loses focus, stops. "I… I guess. I'll try, yeah."

"Okay. Make sure you try really hard."

They come together, and before he even pulls out, she says, "Oh, I think I can feel it inside me." She leans away from him, touches her stomach, smiles. "You made me pregnant! I am so happy it worked. Our baby. The Great TV in the Sky will be so proud!"

He wipes himself off, watches her. "I don't think it works like that," he says. He moves over to the large TV wall, stares into the static. It is just static. He does not see anything in it. No god, no salvation. Nothing. Just black and white and gray spots. This is all bullshit.

"How can you say that?" She frowns at him. She touches her belly again, rubs it. Now she stares into the TV static playing about, loses herself in it. "The Great TV in the Sky spoke to me, just like Father said he would. I know I am pregnant. He told me I would be. He told me I am." She starts crying. "You should not upset me so in my condition. It is not good for the baby."

Jeremy moves away from her. He goes to the door, thinks about leaving. His hand on the doorknob, twisting to open. Eve screams out. It is a scream so full of pain. He turns to face her. She is on the floor, doubled over, holding her belly.

"What's wrong?" Jeremy asks. He does not move away from the door.

"I… I can feel it… growing." The face on her TV screen is scrunched in pain, blurry. She rocks back and forth. Jeremy watches as her stomach balloons out, growing before his eyes.

"You really are pregnant?" He kneels next to her.

She breathes heavily. "I told you The Great TV in the Sky spoke to me. But I did not think it would happen this quickly."

48

"It shouldn't."

She only shrugs at him. The TV static on the wall behind them continues uninterrupted.

"Children aren't born like this. It takes—"

The man in white pushes the door open. Jeremy falls out of the way, scrambles to his feet. But the man in white already has Eve. He scoops her up in his arms, grabbing her under her armpits. She flails to get away. He has too good a grip on her, though. Randall steps into the room behind him. He stands between Jeremy and the man in white. "Take him to his room," the man in white says to Randall. And with this he is gone, Eve with him. Jeremy tries to chase, but Randall pushes him back.

Eve is quiet. She does not say anything as she is led away from her new husband. Her stomach continues to grow.

"Okay, come on then, you heard the Father," Randall says to Jeremy. He gets him out to the hallway. The man in white and Eve have gone the other way. Jeremy looks after them, down the hall.

"Eve," Jeremy calls out. "Eve, please, wait."

She looks back.

Jeremy tries to get away from Randall, but is unable to. He is bigger than Jeremy, stronger, and he has a good grip on Jeremy's arm, his feet planted securely on the ground. "Don't worry, Eve," Jeremy continues. "I will come save you."

Eve and the man in white turn a corner, and she is too far now to hear Jeremy say, "Please, don't worry, I love you." And he really does. It comes out of nowhere, but he knows it to be true.

Randall just laughs at him when he says this. He drags Jeremy the other way, back toward his prison cell room.

Jeremy tries to look back, the way Eve was taken. Randall pushes him forward, smiling.

The door to Jeremy's room is open, a hungry mouth waiting to swallow him. "What are you going to do with her?" he asks.

Randall does not know. He doesn't say anything.

"Please," Jeremy tries. They move closer to his room. "Please, just tell me. Don't hurt her." He thinks about telling him that she is pregnant, but he is sure Randall already knows this. Everyone in this place probably already knows. This is what they have all been waiting for. This is what their church has been all about. This is what their god has promised them.

Jeremy fights it as he is brought closer to his room. He gets his hands on the doorframe and holds on. Randall is in the room already, pulling on him. Jeremy's fingers scream out in pain. He slips, falls into the room. Randall falls with him.

They crumble to the floor in a ball of limbs and flesh. Jeremy jumps on top on Randall, hits him in the face with everything he has. Randall's nose explodes. His head bounces off the floor with a wet thud. Jeremy hits him again and again and again. He leaves him there, bleeding, not moving, but alive. He runs through the halls, passing empty room after empty room. He has no idea where he is going, where Eve was taken. But he knows he has to find her. He has to save his wife and their baby.

Part Three:
The Brain-Dead Idiots

Eve screams out in pain. Her voice echoes through the church, bouncing off the TV screen walls, like it is coming through every speaker at once. The baby is coming, she can feel it moving closer. The members of The Church of TV as God sit on the edge of their seats, watching. They are praying. The man in white tells her to breathe, just breathe—in and out. She does. It hurts. But it also feels good. It feels good to know that she is doing this, that this is all because of her. That it would not be happening without her. She just wishes Jeremy was here with her.

The man in white holds Eve's TV head in his hands. He is standing behind her, whispering prayers over her. She feels as though he really cares for her, a comforting parent. He blesses her with the sign of the TV, blesses his congregation as well. He says, "Do not fight it, my child. It is time. It will be over shortly and all will be as it should. As it says."

Eve screams again. "It... hurts!"

"Do not fight it. Give in to The Great TV in the Sky. Give yourself to Him. He will help you through this. He will make you strong enough to endure."

The TVs around her crackle with a static stronger than ever before. Everyone in the church feels it surge through their bodies. It pulses out through the screens, becomes something tangible in the air around them. The baby is born in a rush of static, placenta lined with wires. Its cries mix with the static in the room, and the sound becomes deafening. Eyes closed, the church members embrace it.

The baby is taken from Eve before she can even see it. She cries out for it. Her TV screen face flickers in shades of deep reds, an explosion behind the glass. She fights against the straps holding her to the gurney next to the flat screen TV altar. The whole thing rocks from side-to-side, but the straps hold. She cannot move.

"Behold," the man in white says, his voice booming, carrying with it everything he has been preaching these past years. Everything he has felt in his heart. Everything he has dreamt. "Our savior has been born."

Eve tries to see the baby, cranes her neck to get a glimpse, just one look. She needs it, needs to see her baby. She cannot. It is right there, so close, but still so far.

"This baby," the man in white continues, "this baby is the reincarnation of The Great TV in the Sky. He has come to us, as the prophecies have predicted, to guide us. He will guide us, and we will follow Him, into heaven, the Land of TVs, where will we live as one—happy and loved—with Him. We will be one, a family. We are Him—The Great TV in the Sky—and He is us."

The congregation chants a soft prayer that Eve cannot make out. The words are lost in the static hissing around her, in the cries of her baby. "Please," she cries. "My baby... please."

The man in white ignores her. She has served her purpose. She is a machine, a catalyst, and now that it is done, she is of no further purpose. Her job is done. Her life is in the hands of The Great TV in the Sky now.

The baby has a TV for a head. Just like his parents. He cries out at the congregation. The little face on his TV screen is nothing but open mouth and squinting eyes, pain and confusion. He has no idea who he is, how important he is. His tiny speakers crackle behind his cries. They are not fully developed yet, cannot handle such force and pressure. The man in white brings the baby back over to the flat screen TV altar, but he does not give him to Eve. A thick orange extension cord runs along the floor next to the altar, back to a large generator. The man in white picks up the end. He makes the sign of the TV over the squirming baby with it and says, "With this cord I give myself unto you, oh Great TV in the Sky." The congregation replies with a heartfelt *Amen,* and the man in white plugs the extension cord into the back of the baby's tiny TV head.

The baby screams out something that sounds more like bad reception that an actual cry. The church is still for a moment, silent. "Please," the man in white says, "my friends, my family, please, plug yourselves in to this baby. Give yourselves over to The Great TV in the Sky. Entrust your bodies and minds to Him." There is rustling throughout the church, as the congregation all reach for their own extension cords. Hundreds of orange cords running the length of the church, under the flat screen TV altar, to the generator. They plug in, everyone stabbing the three prongs into the backs of their necks, into their spinal cords, their brains. This is their sacrifice. There is a small spark in the baby's eyes, behind the still-soft glass of his TV screen face. He lets out another bad reception scream.

The congregation screams to match it. Their eyes flicker to TV static, and the baby falls silent.

The man in white plugs in, feels his skin separating to accept the extension cord that will save him, the three prongs digging into bone and muscle, better than sex. He opens his mouth but no words find their way out. He is lost in the TV static. He sees the baby there, all grown up, sitting amongst all the other TVs in the sky, happy, welcoming. He falls to the ground, on his knees, praying. Blood drips from behind the extension cord in his neck. The blood is the color of TV static.

The Great TV in the Sky is inside every member of The Church of TV as God. They can feel him in there, behind the static in their eyes, weaving his wire fingers into their brains, becoming one with them, taking them over. It is too much for some of the older church members to handle. Their brains will not accept the invasion, the added stimuli.

Most of them fall over dead immediately. Others claw their own eyes out, rip the flesh from their faces, trying to get the static out. They die in puddles of gray blood, screaming next to their loved ones.

It affects others in different ways, The Great TV in the Sky in their heads. The man in white just sits on the floor in front of the flat screen TV altar, his legs crossed, praying. He can feel The Great TV in the Sky moving through his brain. He embraces it, breathes it in. Eve is scared, seeing the congregation change, seeing the static take over their eyes, change the color of their already pale skin, making it even more pale and cold, the color of weak electricity. She bucks against her straps, trying to free herself. She wonders where her husband is, what might be happening to him. She prays that he is safe, and that he will save her from this place. She can still hear his voice, as it echoed through the halls as they were torn apart, telling her not to worry. Saying, "I love you."

A man at the back of the church, hearing a voice in the static in his head, rips his wife's eyeballs out. What spills from the holes in her face is not blood. It is TV static, warm and full of electricity. It drips out in thick clumps, sizzles. The man stares at his wife's eyes in his hand. They stare back at him. He sniffs them, moves them around in his hands, squeezes them. They pop like paintballs. He laps at the warm liquid, licking his hands clean, sucking it all up. TV static drips from his beard. His wife begs him to kill her, she can't take it, just please kill her. But he does not want to kill her. He doesn't even know who she is. He screams nonsense in her face and pushes her away. She stumbles back and trips over a young girl, hisses at her from the ground.

The young girl is Lucy. She is scared and confused and she hates this woman who is hissing at her. Her eyes fizzle, pop. Static crackles in her eardrums. She jumps at the woman, digs her fingers into the soft flesh behind her ears. They fall to the ground, and Lucy shreds the woman's face to ribbons. She bashes the woman's head off the ground until there is nothing left to it, just the two ears in her hands and a puddle of thick, gray and white gore. Lucy sniffs at the mess she made, fishes a clump of meat out of the pile, licks it. A piece of the woman's brain. A thin wire runs through the clump like a vein. Lucy pops it into her mouth and swallows without chewing. She smiles, buries her face into the rest of the mess, and slurps it up. Lucy stops eating, thinks of her mother. She wonders if this mess on the floor in front of her was once her mother. She wonders what a mother even is. The word means nothing to her. She digs another clump of meat out of the puddle on the floor, pops it into her mouth.

A twelve year old boy cannot handle all the static and voices in his head. He does not like this feeling. It's the buzzing deep in his ears. He tries to get it out. Rips his eardrum open, digs around in there with his small fingers, his sharp nails. It does not stop. The static is relentless, the voice of The Great TV in the Sky continues. He attacks the person closest to him, begs her to make it stop. He does not know this person, this thing, is his mother. The mother holds him out at arm's length, looks at his face. She does not see anything she recognizes in it. Only a blank mask, a squirming, soulless demon. It is strange and ugly, and it must be put out of its misery. She slams the boy's ugly face off of the nearest TV seat until it pops open and nothing but TV static comes out. Her husband, the boy's father, sees this. He kneels over the body, drinks the boy's TV static blood. He thinks it will help him remember something, anything. It does not work, and he kills himself in the same way his wife killed their son.

Eve's skin has been rubbed raw against her straps. She bleeds through cracks in her skin. She sees a woman crawling over toward her, toward the altar. The woman is somewhere in her fifties, older but not too old. It is Margaret. Her legs have been crushed. She drags them behind her like dead weight, empty pant legs. TV static drips from her mouth, and most of her teeth have been smashed to jagged shards. She is hissing and drooling and crying.

She makes it to the steps leading up to the altar, reaches out for the man in white sitting there, begs for him to love her without being able to form words in her destroyed mouth. The man in white ignores her. He is too busy praying, trying to speak to The Great TV in the Sky. Margaret tugs on his leg, pulls herself up until she is almost sitting in his lap. Her face inches from his. She leans forward for a kiss, coughs TV static blood in his face.

He looks away from The Great TV in the Sky in his head, meets Margaret's eyes for the first time. He leans toward her now, too, until their noses are touching. She coos something at him, something meant to be soft and loving. He closes his eyes and bites her nose off. She falls back. The man in white chews her nose into a sticky paste, swallows it. Margaret screams noises at him. He does not understand her.

She sticks her hand into the hole where her nose had been, feels around in there. The skin around the hole splits apart, making room for her fingers, now in past the knuckles. It tears away in meaty flaps. She rips the flaps the rest of the way. Her face is not a face anymore, just a thick, bony mess. She tosses the scraps of her face at the man in white. He catches a few of them and slurps them into his mouth, does not enjoy it.

Eve sees all of this, cries harder. "Jeremy," she cries, trying and failing to keep her voice to a whisper, "where are you? Jeremy?" She screams it out now. "*Jeremy!*" Over and over. The congregation of The Church of TV as God stops what they at doing at the sound of her screams. They turn to her. Their TV static eyes all focus on her.

Jeremy makes his way through the hallways, constantly looking back over his shoulder, expecting Randall to be there chasing him. The place is quiet, empty. He gets a bad feeling, a buzz in the antennas sticking out of the top on his TV head. Something is wrong, and he needs to find Eve.

He continues walking hallway after hallway. All of them look exactly the same, like he is just walking circles. And then out of the silence he hears the distinct shout-bark of Benjamin. He wonders what the people here have been doing to him. He remembers the way the dog looked, all beaten and bloody, in the van, when they were brought here. He wonders where the barks are coming from. Goes to a window and looks outside, at the world beyond the church.

Benjamin is out there, tied to a tree in the decrepit yard behind the dormitory

Jeremy pulls the window open, looks around him one last time before sticking his head out. The room he's in is empty, an unused bed, a bare mattress, an empty closet. Jeremy hangs out the window and shouts to get Benjamin's attention. The dog screams out, wagging his tail at Jeremy, greeting him like a friendly voice in a foreign land. Jeremy looks down. He's three floors up, too high to jump. "Hold on," he says to Benjamin, "stay there. I'll find another way down."

He slips back in the room and hears Benjamin shout, "Where the hell else am I going to go? I'm tied to a fucking—"

Jeremy finds his way outside and unties Benjamin. As they are turning away from the tree, back toward the building, the door behind them bursts open. Randall stands in the doorway, blood dripping down his chin like a sloppy red beard. His gray robe is soaked with it. He is breathing heavy, snarling almost.

"Your doing?" Benjamin asks, nodding over to Randall.

Jeremy nods.

"Nice work, man, didn't think you'd have anything like that in you."

"Well, I do," Jeremy says, short. "Long story, no time to—"

But Randall is already charging them. Benjamin barks twice, a warning. Randall keeps coming, an unstoppable force. Benjamin squats low, hair standing up. He growls. He recognizes Randall from the cemetery. He remembers Randall as the one who beat him.

Benjamin leaps into the air, meets Randall as he approaches. "You sick son of a bitch," he growls, sinking his teeth into the flabby skin at Randall's neck. He tears a chunk off, blood sprays out like a faucet. "You like beating poor, innocent puppies?" He goes back for more neck fat. Chews, growls, barks. Randall falls to the ground, flailing around, trying to shake the dog off, trying to apologize, to beg forgiveness, his tears mixed with the blood on his face. But Benjamin holds tighter, doesn't care about Randall's begging. He goes for the throat, his animal instinct kicking in. He tears skin and meat and fat away from Randall's body, his fur thick with red-black blood. Randall's body goes limp. He soils his robe and chokes on blood. Benjamin digs his snout further into Randall's neck, chews on his throat, crushes his windpipe. Randall lets out one final cry and dies in a pool of his own blood. But Benjamin keeps going, keeps chewing, keeps calling Randall's corpse a mother fucker between bites.

Jeremy grabs Benjamin by the scruff of his neck and pulls him away. Benjamin, full of tunnel vision and rage, snaps at Jeremy, almost catches him with bloodied fangs. Jeremy drops the dog, and it seems to jar him back to the real world, away from Randall. He looks around, looks up at Jeremy, sad and sorry. His eyes saying he'll be a good boy, now. An innocent looking dog covered in blood and chunks of meat, chunks of Randall.

Jeremy starts running back around to the front of the building. Benjamin follows, calling, "Why the good god damn are you going back, man, let's just get the fuck out of here?"

"Can't," is all Jeremy says. He turns the corner. There is the church. Small and nondescript, just like any church anywhere in the country. Pointed roof, large stained glass windows. It's only when you get close to the windows that you notice that they show pictures of TVs and remote control angels. The Great TV in the Sky. Scenes from the Holy TV Guide.

"Fuck that. These people kidnapped us, beat us. We have the chance to go, and we need to jump on that shit. We need to go. Fuck revenge or whatever you're thinking. Just stick that non-existent tail between your legs and let's fucking go. We'll call the cops. Let them deal with this."

"We can't," Jeremy says again. He does not stop moving.

"Why the fuck not?"

"I told you—it's a long story. You can leave if you want. I won't hold it against you. Just go."

"I'm not gonna leave you alone to do something stupid and get yourself killed, no," Benjamin huffs. "Just give me the short version then, man," he says, catching up, a loyal companion. "I'm not running back into this fucking place without knowing why I'm doing it or what I'm getting myself into."

"My wife is in there."

"What do you mean your wife is in there?"

"Exactly what I said."

"But you don't have a wife. Shit, a few days ago you were just saying that you haven't been laid in years. Now you have a wife."

"Let's get one thing straight," Jeremy says. "You were the one that said I haven't been laid in years. I said no such thing."

"Okay, whatever. But you have a wife now? How the fuck does that even happen?"

"That's the long part of the story. All that matters is that they kidnapped her and I have to get her back. She's about to have a baby."

"Whoa, man, whoa. You married a pregnant chick? Kinda stupid, you ask me, getting tied down to some bitch about to have pups."

"No, she wasn't pregnant before... it's mine... My baby."

"Wait, how—"

"No idea," Jeremy cuts in, knowing the question, knowing there is no rational explanation for it. "I know it doesn't make sense. It doesn't matter. I'm turning into a TV. You're a talking dog. I married a woman with a TV for a head and she went from being un-pregnant to very pregnant in just a few short minutes. Everything is all fucked up. Nothing makes sense. Can we just move on?"

They are standing outside of the church. They hear sounds, voices coming from under the door, behind the windows. With it, a bright light that flickers and pops like lightning flashes. The voices are frenzied, panicked.

"Okay," Benjamin says, taking a step away from the door, sniffing the air in its direction, "what the fuck is going on in there?" He looks to Jeremy for an answer, sees nothing there.

Jeremy, with nothing better to do, no other real options, tries the door. It is locked. He thinks about knocking, but all the screaming and suckling sounds coming from inside make him think twice about it. "We need to find another way in," he says, more to himself than to Benjamin.

Benjamin takes it upon himself to get them inside. "I've got it," he says, all business. Jeremy ignores him, stares up at the second floor, if there's a way to climb in through an upper window to get inside. He doesn't notice Benjamin walking up to one of the large stained glass windows depicting The Great TV in the Sky riding a flaming chariot down to Earth in a representation of the second coming. He also does not notice the rock Benjamin is holding in his mouth.

Benjamin says something around the rock, "Get ready, here we go," but Jeremy doesn't hear it. It just sounds like growling. He throws his head to the side, releases the rock. It shatters the window, colored glass exploding like a fireworks display. He stands there as glass shards fall around him, thinking about how the tough guys in the action movies he used to watch with his former roommates never ran away from explosions—they just stand there all cool, all badass, and they are never hurt, the explosions just move around them, out of their way. He watches the shards come at him. They are not moving around him. They get tangled in his already bloodied fur, cutting him up. He runs away, fighting back a whimper.

Jeremy jumps back at the sound of glass shattering. He looks at Benjamin. Benjamin seems to shrug—if dogs are capable of shrugging.

Benjamin says, "Got us in, right?"

Jeremy doesn't say anything. He looks into the hole in the window, sees what all the sounds were. Sees members of The Church of TV as God fighting and killing each other and crying and kissing and fucking, all covered in a thick gray liquid. Some are sitting perfectly still, staring at the wall in front of them, or staring at the floor. Combing their shaved heads with invisible combs. They are laughing. Giggling. Screaming. One man is walking into a wall over and over again like he can't figure out why he can't get past it. A baby sucks on a severed toe. They are picking their noses, picking other people's noses. Some are missing limbs or teeth or eyes. A woman is missing the bottom half of her jaw. Her tongue flops around like a dead snake. They are all eating, chewing.

He does not see Eve anywhere. She is at the front of the church, hidden behind a blockade of bodies. The man in white is licking her TV screen face. He is drooling Margaret's gray blood all over her.

Jeremy moves closer to the window, trying to find his wife in the melee. For the first time, he notices the eyes of the people inside the church, that they are the color of TV static. Gray and swirling like a snowstorm, spreading out from their eyeballs, taking over the rest of their faces.

"What. The. Fuck?" Benjamin says, speaking for the both of them. "What the... are they... son of a..."

"Something is wrong," Jeremy offers. Benjamin responds with a *no shit* grumble. Benjamin says, "It's like... they're... I guess TV really does rot your brain." He laughs. He sniffs the air again, looks grossed out and scared by what he smells.

Jeremy looks at the dog.

"I mean, think about it. They're, like, brain-dead idiots." He flicks his nose at a man sitting at the back of the church. "Look at that one over there. His doesn't seem to understand his hand. Like what it's doing connected to his wrist. Like he doesn't know it's *his* hand."

They watch the man try to pull his hand away from the wrist with his other hand. When this doesn't work, he starts chewing on the wrist, tearing the flesh away to rid himself of the unwanted appendage.

"This is fucked up."

Jeremy doesn't say anything. He is too busy watching a teenager that is watching him. The kid moves closer, sniffing the air. His eyes leak gray liquid. All of the other church members stop what they are doing, too. They look over to Jeremy and Benjamin standing there in the glassless window, like they are on TV. The TV man on TV. The brain-dead idiots all make the same hiss-crackle with their gray, dripping mouths.

"Oh, mother fuck this," Benjamin says. He turns to run. Jeremy stays behind, not moving, just watching.

The brain-dead idiots of The Church of TV as God surge forward, moving to the window, wanting the TV man, needing to get to him. But not knowing why.

In all the movement, Jeremy spots Eve up at the front of the church, sees that she is tied to some kind of table.

Brain-dead idiots still move around her, but their attention is now focused on Jeremy. Except for one, on top of her, his face in hers. He watches Eve try to shake the man off of her, try to wiggle out from under her captor. But she can't get free, can't move, the straps holding her in place. She lets out a scream but Jeremy can't hear it over all the other screaming.

Jeremy can't get to her. The brain-dead idiots are crowding the window, reaching out for him through the hole. Blocking him from his wife. From Eve.

They crawl through the hole in the window, two, three at a time. Their already mangled bodies cut to pieces on the jagged shards of colored glass sticking up from the window frame. They do not seem to notice or care; they lick the gray blood from themselves and the people around them. Their focus on only Jeremy, so close to him they can see their reflections in his TV screen face.

The man in white straddles Eve. He continues to lick her TV screen face, over and over again, from bottom to top. A thick line of sloppy goop runs the path of his tongue. His eyes are black and white and gray. "Please," Eve tries. "Please stop… Let me go."

He does not answer.

Eve has shifted in her ties. She can see her baby lying perfectly still on the flat screen TV altar near her.

The man in white pulls his dick out from under his robe. It is thin and small and mostly erect. A small pearl of gray-white drips from the tip. He moves over to Eve. She is still naked, tied with her legs spread for child birth. Inches away now, the man in white mumbling to himself, saying prayers, blesses himself with the sign of the TV. The TV baby cries out.

Eve holds her breath.

The man in white stops moving, looks over to the baby.

The baby coughs, gurgles, through the tiny speakers at the base of his TV head.

The man in white goes to the baby. Its eyes are open. They are clear and red and seem to be looking directly into the man in white. They see everything, burning so bright he has to look away. The TV walls around them flicker to life, show nothing. Only static, more static. This is The Great TV in the Sky. The man in white knows it. He whispers, "I am sorry, my lord, I have—"

The static-hiss on the TV intensifies, cuts him off. It gets so loud, it is all he can hear. All he can think about. There is nothing but the static. The flat screen TV altar opens up and the baby falls down into the screen, disappears there. The static lightning bolts into the man in white's head, and everything around him goes black.

A crying baby wakes him up. It is dark, and he comes to in a puddle of his own blood. He seems to be bleeding from just about everywhere, covered in it. Only it is not blood. It is too full of energy, electricity. Things around him come into focus and he sees that it is liquefied TV static, not blood. He tries to back away from the growing, pulsing puddle, but he cannot move very far. He is in a very small room. He hits the back wall. He holds his hand out in front of him and it thunks against the inside of a TV screen.

He is trapped inside of a TV, his image displayed hundreds of times on all the TVs making up The Church of TV as God. He thinks that maybe this is where he is supposed to be, that this place will lead him to heaven. The Great TV in the Sky will come for him.

A voice laughs in his head. The baby's laugh. The laugh of the reincarnation of The Great TV in the Sky. The man in white tries to scream, but his voice does not escape all of the speakers of his prison. Only he can hear it. The TVs have all been muted.

Eve watches hundreds of copies of the man in white silently scream around her. He is banging on the insides of the TV screens. The walls around her shake. She cries and cries and pulls against her restraints. She begs for Jeremy.

Jeremy and Benjamin run around to the back of the church, through the alley. The crackling horde stampedes behind them, moving as one. A few miles down, they come to the back door of a bar. They slip inside and move through the darkness.

The place is quiet and empty. The bartender stands behind the bar pointing a remote control at a TV hanging in the corner. The screen only shows static. It gets all jumbled up, sounds of crackling voices coming through the speaker.

"Now what in the hell—" the man says, slapping the remote into his open hand. He sees Jeremy and Benjamin come up behind him. "Holy hell," he stutter-shouts. "Where the hell did y'all come from?" He seems to notice Jeremy for the first time, sees his misshapen head. "Whoa, boy, what the hell is wrong with ya?"

"That's not very fucking nice, man," Benjamin says. "Didn't your mother ever teach you not to stare at other people's deformities? Not to bring attention to them? You just look away and pretend they're not there. That's what you're supposed to do. Don't you think my friend here knows he's all fucked up looking? You don't have to point it out. Keep reminding him and shit."

The bartender is now staring at Benjamin, a talking dog. "Okay, now, just what in the hell is going on here? This some kinda fuckin' joke? Billy put ya up to it?"

"Who the hell is Billy?" Benjamin says. "No man, this is not a fucking joke. Does it look like one?"

The man shrugs.

Jeremy walks over to the window, to see if the brain-dead idiots are out there. "Y'all from that church?" the bartender asks. "I thought I told ya crazies to stay out of my place. After the last time, I don't want no more troub—"

"No," Jeremy says. He turns to face the bartender, the dull neon bar lights reflecting off his TV screen face. "We are not from that church. We are trying to get away from them. They are after us."

Benjamin jumps in. "They want to get my man, here." He flicks his nose at Jeremy. "They think he's like God or some shit. It's understandable, maybe. I mean, he is turning into a fucking TV after all. And they seem to be nutty for some TV."

The bartender turns away from them, grabs a bottle of whiskey and a shot glass. Thinks twice about it and just chugs from the bottle. "I'll have one of those, too, thanks," Benjamin says. The man starts to protest, thinks about it, and just shrugs. He grabs a bowl of peanuts off the bar, dumps it out, and pours the whiskey into it. Benjamin laps at the whiskey happily.

The bartender watches him, smiles a bit. He thinks about his own dog. Wonders what she would say if she could talk. He looks back to Jeremy. "They after ya, huh?"

Jeremy nods.

"Them some crazy fuckers. Worshipping TV and shit. What kinda fuckin' nonsense is that? They more a cult than anything. Police can't do nothin' 'bout 'em though. They ain't technically done nothin' wrong."

"They kidnapped my wife," Jeremy says. "She was pregnant."

The bartender just nods, like that's all he needs to hear. He finally has the proof he needs to get the crazies locked up. He goes over to the phone, picks it up. Before he starts to dial, the TV screen over him explodes, raining glass and sparks down on him. He falls out of the way. The phone clatters to the floor, rips away from the wall. The brain-dead idiots crash through the windows, the doors, the walls. They come from everywhere. They crowd into the room, not doing anything. They watch Jeremy. They wait for him.

The bartender stands up, holding a shotgun. "Y'all better get the fuck outta here," he calls, swinging the gun around the room, as if to say he could shoot any one of them, all of them. If they'd just give him a reason.

The brain-dead idiots turn their attention on the bartender. Their voices crackle-pop as one. They breathe as one, share one consciousness.

"Go on," he shouts. "Git!"

The two brain-dead idiots closest to the bartender make the first move. One—a man with half of his face busted open, spilling gray blood—grabs for his gun. The bartender struggles with him, and a middle-aged woman, naked and covered in gore, jumps on him. She spits and drools TV static all over the bartender. She rips his clothes off and snuggles her body up against his. The bartender looks scared, looks to Jeremy for help. Jeremy does not move. The woman, bored with cuddling, rakes her nails up and down the bartender's bare stomach, digging in deeper with each pass, until he is cut up and bleeding all over. She seems confused by the deep red of his blood. She sniffs at it on her fingers, tastes it. The other brain-dead idiots just stand there, frozen, watching.

She thrusts both hands into the bartender's stomach, moves them around, pulls out handfuls of intestine. She tosses them at the man with half a face. He embraces them like a warm shower.

The bartender's body twitches. He tries to scream, but two more brain-dead idiots have moved in on him. They are clawing at his face, pulling his lips apart. A little girl chews the tongue out of his mouth, and the rest surge forward.

Jeremy and Benjamin use this distraction to sneak out the front door. They run as fast as they can through the streets. The streets are empty, a few cars stopped here and there, doors open, engines running. Everything covered in blood, sticky and pungent.

Inside the houses and apartments they pass, TV static glows through the darkness. Brain-dead idiots come out of the houses. People turned into brain-dead idiots. Their TVs infecting them. They crackle-hiss at Benjamin and Jeremy. "The car, there," Benjamin shouts, as the street fills up with more and more of them.

Jeremy and Benjamin climb into the idling car, a taxi. The cab driver—getting a cup of coffee to make it through the rest of his shift, knowing nothing of what is happening to the city around him—rushes out after Jeremy peels away in his car. The man chases them down the street until he feels a sharp stab in his lungs. He is too out of shape to continue chasing them. He stands, panting and clutching his chest, at the corner, watching as his cab speeds away from him. He hears a noise coming up behind him, turns to face it, and is knocked to the ground by a few dozen brain-dead idiots. He is ripped to pieces before he can even scream. They drink his blood, play with his body, and continue after the TV man.

Jeremy steers the car back toward the church. "Oh, hell no, man," Benjamin sighs. "We're going back to that fucking place... again?"

Jeremy doesn't take his eyes off the road. "I need to get Eve."

There are more and more stopped cars this way, more bodies in the street the closer they get to the church. More brain-dead idiots are stumbling about, completely unaware of what is going on around them. They are sniffing things, tasting things, chewing. The world is so new to them, everything is a mystery. They follow the car with their TV static eyes, as it passes. They try to grab it, can't understand the distance between them and it. They follow.

A small TV in the back of the cab jitter-flickers. It normally shows commercials and fun trivia facts about the city and its monuments or accomplishments. But now it only shows static. The man in white can be seen behind the static, covered in soupy gore. He is banging against the screen, crying out silent words. A baby skitters across the screen. Jeremy and Benjamin do not see this. They are both in the front seat.

"This chick better be worth it," Benjamin says. He is playing cool, acting hard. But Jeremy can tell he is worried, a little scared.

"It'll be okay," Jeremy says, doesn't know if he believes it himself. He reaches out and pets the dog's head.

The Church of TV as God shows itself in the distance. It stands in the darkness like a tumor, strange gray light glowing through the stained glass windows, surrounding it like an aura. Coming up the road, they see a massive horde of these people, the brain-dead idiots. They stretch across the street, from building to building, blocking the path, walking slow. There must be close to a thousand, their minds all linked together. Church members and civilians. The collective glow of their TV static eyes lights up the night like a full moon hanging low over the city.

Jeremy slams on the brakes.

Benjamin says, "Son. Of. A. Bitch." He looks all around them, his doggie brain working overtime for something, anything. He only comes up with one solution. "*Floor it!*" he screams.

"But..." Jeremy starts, thinks about it. There is nothing else. He presses the pedal down as far as it will go, trying for more. The tires squeal, smoke. The car shoots forward. It reaches the horde in seconds. The first few rows of brain-dead idiots explode in a spray of blood and TV static, arms and legs, organs. Some jump out of the way. Others jump in front of the car, sacrificing themselves in an attempt to stop the car. For the greater good. It does not work. They are crushed. They reach out for the car, grab on to anything they can get their hands on—the side mirrors, door frames, wheel wells, bumper, the On Duty sign suction-cupped to the roof. Jeremy takes them for a ride, swerving to shake them off. They hold tight, fingers ripping into metal.

They get to the church, brain-dead idiots still clinging to the car. The car crashes into the side of the building, crushing two brain-dead idiots that had been holding on to the front bumper. The gray light pours through the windows like thick smoke. It smells of raw meat and electricity, like a lightning storm, a burnt-out appliance. Jeremy runs inside, straight to Eve, still tied to the flat screen TV altar. Brain-dead idiots move in behind them, slowly, cautiously. Like they know this is a sacred place.

Jeremy unties Eve.

"The baby," Eve cries. She throws her arms around Jeremy, rests her TV head in the space between his TV and his shoulder.

"Where is it?" Jeremy asks. He does not know if his baby is a boy or a girl.

The brain-dead idiots crowd around them, moving about the church. They all bless themselves with the sign of

71

the TV at the same time, their hands moving as one. They blink together.

Eve cowers against Jeremy at the sight of them. Benjamin barks at them, swears at them. Eve feels safe with Jeremy. She points to the TV screen walls. The hundreds of screens that make up the interior of The Church of TV as God all show the same thing: the man in white huddled up in the fetal position. His TV static eyes are missing. He has clawed them out. And a thick gray mess drips from the newly opened holes. The TV baby runs from one screen to the next, laughing, giggling. His tiny TV screen mimics the man in white's terrified face.

"Baby, please," Eve calls out, moving closer to the wall of TVs.

The baby stops skittering across the screens, stares out.

The man in white hears this, feels them out there watching him. He crawls closer to the screen. He pounds his bloody fists against it, begs to be let out. His words are not heard. Every screen has the same yellow word written in the bottom corner: MUTE. The baby returns his attention to his prisoner. He approaches one of the images. The man in white crawls away from the baby, hits the back wall. He holds his hands out in front of his face, in surrender.

The baby skitter-crawls up the man in white's chest. He burrows his TV head deep into his stomach, crawls inside.

The man in white's body bulges and expands as the baby moves around, making his way up to the brain.

The brain-dead idiots stare at the TV screens, watching the baby, their savior, work his way through the man in white's body. They breathe heavily, together in and out. They sit on the TV seats out in the church.

The baby explodes through the top of the man in white's head. Bone and skin split away like torn paper. The baby soars up and out like a butterfly from a cocoon, covered in thick TV static mucus.

The man in white dies the same way in hundreds of different TV screens. His corpse dissolves into a puddle of gray and black static-pus.

The baby is only visible in one of the TV screens. He looks out at the church, at his parents. His TV screen shows a smiling face. He crawls around again, from screen to screen.

Eve moves over to the baby, follows him around the screens. She touches the screen, feels nothing but cold glass.

"That was fucked up, dude," Benjamin says. "That baby straight up murdered that guy. Like seriously."

"That's my son," Jeremy says, smiling.

"Fucked up," Benjamin repeats.

"How do we get him out of there?" Eve asks, still following the baby. He is now all the way at the top, crawling back and forth along the back wall. "Jeremy, help... please."

"I'll think of something."

A wave of whispering voices washes over them. They are coming from the brain-dead idiots, the members of The Church of TV as God.

"What they fuck are they—"

"Praying," Jeremy says, cutting Benjamin off.

"It's pretty creepy."

Great TV in the Sky, forgive us our sins... they pray. They stare up at the baby crawling around the TVs. The baby waves out at the people, his followers. They plug themselves back into the generator, into the one extension cord that disappears into the flat screen TV altar. The static in their eyes shrinks to a single dot, and then goes black, shutting down. They lean forward, lifeless, frozen in prayer. Their bodies crumble to gray and black dust.

The TV baby sits inside a wall of TV screens, close to the floor. He laughs and watches the dog run back and forth throughout what was The Church of TV as God. The dog chases a ball. He catches the ball and brings it back to the man with the large TV head. Behind him a woman sweeps up gray and black dust into large piles. She also has a TV for a head.

"That was a good one," Benjamin says, "but I caught the shit out of that motherfucker."

Eve smiles, watching the two of them.

Jeremy's TV screen face lights up. Laughter comes from his speakers. "Where'd you get this ball anyway?" he asks Benjamin.

"I found it in one of the rooms, while I was investigating the other day."

"You really shouldn't go through their rooms."

"Why the hell not? It's not like they're coming back for their shit."

Jeremy half-shrugs, agrees. He throws the ball again.

Benjamin chases it. "Come back here, asshole," he shouts after it.

The baby laughs again.

"I think I will call him Felix," Eve says. She looks over to the baby, waves and smiles.

"Felix, why Felix?"

"Why not Felix? Felix is a powerful name. I love it. It is beautiful, and he is beautiful. Everything right now is beautiful."

"Felix," Jeremy says again. He looks over at the baby. "Do you think he'll ever come out of there?"

Eve sets her broom down, sits on the edge of a TV seat. "Probably not," she says, matter-of-factly. "He is happy in there... At least I think he is. Anyway, he will come out when he is ready. Until then, we will be here with him. For him. We are a family."

Benjamin comes trotting back over with the ball in his mouth. He drops it. "Wait, wait, wait," he says. "We're going to stay here with him?" He looks back over at the baby, at Felix. "As in: live here?"

Jeremy shrugs. "Why not?"

"Uh, because hundreds of people just died here, in this very room like two days ago, just turned to dust like *poof*. And, currently, your wife is sweeping that people-dust up. That's fucked up, if you ask me. Plus this place is probably haunted and shit."

"It'll be okay," Jeremy says. He picks the ball up and throws it again. It bounces off the TV wall across the church. Benjamin chases it, barking. Baby Felix crawls across the TV wall, trying to make it to the ball first. Benjamin gets it, runs it back and forth in front of the TVs, taunting baby Felix.

"Do you really want to stay here?" Jeremy asks Eve.

"Of course," she says. "Where else would we go? Our family is here. This is our home."

"I don't—"

"Just give it some time, with a little bit of work, a womanly touch, this place will be great. Plus..." she lets her words fall away, rubs her stomach in a way that can only mean one thing.

"But... how? I mean when?"

She just smiles at him, wide-eyed. She does not know, thinks: *The Great TV in the Sky works in mysterious ways.*

Daniel Vlasaty lives in Chicago with his wife and two cats. He works at a methadone clinic. He likes many things and has a few hobbies.

The Church of TV as God is his first book.

BIZARRO BOOKS

CATALOG   SPRING 2013

ERASERHEAD PRESS

Your major resource for the bizarro fiction genre:

WWW.BIZARROCENTRAL.COM

Introduce yourselves to the bizarro fiction genre and all of its authors with the Bizarro Starter Kit series. Each volume features short novels and short stories by ten of the leading bizarro authors, designed to give you a perfect sampling of the genre for only $10.

BB-0X1
"The Bizarro Starter Kit"
(Orange)

Featuring D. Harlan Wilson, Carlton Mellick III, Jeremy Robert Johnson, Kevin L Donihe, Gina Ranalli, Andre Duza, Vincent W. Sakowski, Steve Beard, John Edward Lawson, and Bruce Taylor.
236 pages $10

BB-0X2
"The Bizarro Starter Kit"
(Blue)

Featuring Ray Fracalossy, Jeremy C. Shipp, Jordan Krall, Mykle Hansen, Andersen Prunty, Eckhard Gerdes, Bradley Sands, Steve Aylett, Christian TeBordo, and Tony Rauch. **244 pages $10**

BB-0X2
"The Bizarro Starter Kit"
(Purple)

Featuring Russell Edson, Athena Villaverde, David Agranoff, Matthew Revert, Andrew Goldfarb, Jeff Burk, Garrett Cook, Kris Saknussemm, Cody Goodfellow, and Cameron Pierce **264 pages $10**

BB-001 "The Kafka Effekt" D. Harlan Wilson — A collection of forty-four irreal short stories loosely written in the vein of Franz Kafka, with more than a pinch of William S. Burroughs sprinkled on top. **211 pages $14**

BB-002 "Satan Burger" Carlton Mellick III — The cult novel that put Carlton Mellick III on the map ... Six punks get jobs at a fast food restaurant owned by the devil in a city violently overpopulated by surreal alien cultures. **236 pages $14**

BB-003 "Some Things Are Better Left Unplugged" Vincent Sakwoski — Join The Man and his Nemesis, the obese tabby, for a nightmare roller coaster ride into this postmodern fantasy. **152 pages $10**

BB-005 "Razor Wire Pubic Hair" Carlton Mellick III — A genderless humandildo is purchased by a razor dominatrix and brought into her nightmarish world of bizarre sex and mutilation. **176 pages $11**

BB-007 "The Baby Jesus Butt Plug" Carlton Mellick III — Using clones of the Baby Jesus for anal sex will be the hip sex fetish of the future. **92 pages $10**

BB-010 "The Menstruating Mall" Carlton Mellick III — "The Breakfast Club meets Chopping Mall as directed by David Lynch." - Brian Keene **212 pages $12**

BB-011 "Angel Dust Apocalypse" Jeremy Robert Johnson — Meth-heads, man-made monsters, and murderous Neo-Nazis. "Seriously amazing short stories..." - Chuck Palahniuk, author of Fight Club **184 pages $11**

BB-015 "Foop!" Chris Genoa — Strange happenings are going on at Dactyl, Inc, the world's first and only time travel tourism company.
"A surreal pie in the face!" - Christopher Moore **300 pages $14**

BB-032 "Extinction Journals" Jeremy Robert Johnson — An uncanny voyage across a newly nuclear America where one man must confront the problems associated with loneliness, insane dieties, radiation, love, and an ever-evolving cockroach suit with a mind of its own. **104 pages $10**

BB-037 "The Haunted Vagina" Carlton Mellick III — It's difficult to love a woman whose vagina is a gateway to the world of the dead. **132 pages $10**

BB-043 "War Slut" Carlton Mellick III — Part "1984," part "Waiting for Godot," and part action horror video game adaptation of John Carpenter's "The Thing." **116 pages $10**

BB-047 "Sausagey Santa" Carlton Mellick III — A bizarro Christmas tale featuring Santa as a piratey mutant with a body made of sausages. **124 pages $10**

BB-048 "Misadventures in a Thumbnail Universe" Vincent Sakowski — Dive deep into the surreal and satirical realms of neo-classical Blender Fiction, filled with television shoes and flesh-filled skies. **120 pages $10**

BB-053 "Ballad of a Slow Poisoner" Andrew Goldfarb — Millford Mutterwurst sat down on a Tuesday to take his afternoon tea, and made the unpleasant discovery that his elbows were becoming flatter. **128 pages $10**

BB-055 "Help! A Bear is Eating Me" Mykle Hansen — The bizarro, heartwarming, magical tale of poor planning, hubris and severe blood loss... **150 pages $11**

BB-056 "Piecemeal June" Jordan Krall — A man falls in love with a living sex doll, but with love comes danger when her creator comes after her with crab-squid assassins. **90 pages $9**

BB-058 "The Overwhelming Urge" Andersen Prunty — A collection of bizarro tales by Andersen Prunty. **150 pages $11**

BB-059 "Adolf in Wonderland" Carlton Mellick III — A dreamlike adventure that takes a young descendant of Adolf Hitler's design and sends him down the rabbit hole into a world of imperfection and disorder. **180 pages $11**

BB-061 "Ultra Fuckers" Carlton Mellick III — Absurdist suburban horror about a couple who enter an upper middle class gated community but can't find their way out. **108 pages $9**

BB-062 "House of Houses" Kevin L. Donihe — An odd man wants to marry his house. Unfortunately, all of the houses in the world collapse at the same time in the Great House Holocaust. Now he must travel to House Heaven to find his departed fiancee. **172 pages $11**

BB-064 "Squid Pulp Blues" Jordan Krall — In these three bizarro-noir novellas, the reader is thrown into a world of murderers, drugs made from squid parts, deformed gun-toting veterans, and a mischievous apocalyptic donkey. **204 pages $12**

BB-065 "Jack and Mr. Grin" Andersen Prunty — "When Mr. Grin calls you can hear a smile in his voice. Not a warm and friendly smile, but the kind that seizes your spine in fear. You don't need to pay your phone bill to hear it. That smile is in every line of Prunty's prose." - Tom Bradley. **208 pages $12**

BB-066 "Cybernetrix" Carlton Mellick III — What would you do if your normal everyday world was slowly mutating into the video game world from Tron? **212 pages $12**

BB-072 "Zerostrata" Andersen Prunty — Hansel Nothing lives in a tree house, suffers from memory loss, has a very eccentric family, and falls in love with a woman who runs naked through the woods every night. **144 pages $11**

BB-073 "The Egg Man" Carlton Mellick III — It is a world where humans reproduce like insects. Children are the property of corporations, and having an enormous ten-foot brain implanted into your skull is a grotesque sexual fetish. Mellick's industrial urban dystopia is one of his darkest and grittiest to date. **184 pages $11**

BB-074 "Shark Hunting in Paradise Garden" Cameron Pierce — A group of strange humanoid religious fanatics travel back in time to the Garden of Eden to discover it is invested with hundreds of giant flying maneating sharks. **150 pages $10**

BB-075 "Apeshit" Carlton Mellick III - Friday the 13th meets Visitor Q. Six hipster teens go to a cabin in the woods inhabited by a deformed killer. An incredibly fucked-up parody of B-horror movies with a bizarro slant. **192 pages $12**

BB-076 "Fuckers of Everything on the Crazy Shitting Planet of the Vomit At mosphere" Mykle Hansen - Three bizarro satires. Monster Cocks, Journey to the Center of Agnes Cuddlebottom, and Crazy Shitting Planet. **228 pages $12**

BB-077 "The Kissing Bug" Daniel Scott Buck — In the tradition of Roald Dahl, Tim Burton, and Edward Gorey, comes this bizarro anti-war children's story about a bohemian conenose kissing bug who falls in love with a human woman. **116 pages $10**

BB-078 "MachoPoni" Lotus Rose — It's My Little Pony... *Bizarro* style! A long time ago Poniworld was split in two. On one side of the Jagged Line is the Pastel Kingdom, a magical land of music, parties, and positivity. On the other side of the Jagged Line is Dark Kingdom inhabited by an army of undead ponies. **148 pages $11**

BB-079 "The Faggiest Vampire" Carlton Mellick III — A Roald Dahl-esque children's story about two faggy vampires who partake in a mustache competition to find out which one is truly the faggiest. **104 pages $10**

BB-080 "Sky Tongues" Gina Ranalli — The autobiography of Sky Tongues, the biracial hermaphrodite actress with tongues for fingers. Follow her strange life story as she rises from freak to fame. **204 pages $12**

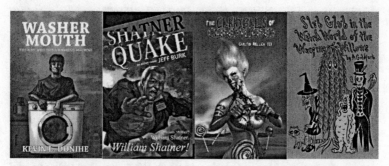

BB-081 **"Washer Mouth" Kevin L. Donihe** - A washing machine becomes human and pursues his dream of meeting his favorite soap opera star. **244 pages $11**

BB-082 **"Shatnerquake" Jeff Burk** - All of the characters ever played by William Shatner are suddenly sucked into our world. Their mission: hunt down and destroy the real William Shatner. **100 pages $10**

BB-083 **"The Cannibals of Candyland" Carlton Mellick III** - There exists a race of cannibals that are made of candy. They live in an underground world made out of candy. One man has dedicated his life to killing them all. **170 pages $11**

BB-084 **"Slub Glub in the Weird World of the Weeping Willows"** **Andrew Goldfarb** - The charming tale of a blue glob named Slub Glub who helps the weeping willows whose tears are flooding the earth. There are also hyenas, ghosts, and a voodoo priest **100 pages $10**

BB-085 **"Super Fetus" Adam Pepper** - Try to abort this fetus and he'll kick your ass! **104 pages $10**

BB-086 **"Fistful of Feet" Jordan Krall** - A bizarro tribute to spaghetti westerns, featuring Cthulhu-worshipping Indians, a woman with four feet, a crazed gunman who is obsessed with sucking on candy, Syphilis-ridden mutants, sexually transmitted tattoos, and a house devoted to the freakiest fetishes. **228 pages $12**

BB-087 **"Ass Goblins of Auschwitz" Cameron Pierce** - It's Monty Python meets Nazi exploitation in a surreal nightmare as can only be imagined by Bizarro author Cameron Pierce. **104 pages $10**

BB-088 **"Silent Weapons for Quiet Wars" Cody Goodfellow** - "This is high-end psychological surrealist horror meets bottom-feeding low-life crime in a techno-thrilling science fiction world full of Lovecraft and magic..." -John Skipp **212 pages $12**

BB-089 "Warrior Wolf Women of the Wasteland" Carlton Mellick III — Road Warrior Werewolves versus McDonaldland Mutants...post-apocalyptic fiction has never been quite like this. **316 pages $13**

BB-091 "Super Giant Monster Time" Jeff Burk — A tribute to choose your own adventures and Godzilla movies. Will you escape the giant monsters that are rampaging the fuck out of your city and shit? Or will you join the mob of alien-controlled punk rockers causing chaos in the streets? What happens next depends on you. **188 pages $12**

BB-092 "Perfect Union" Cody Goodfellow — "Cronenberg's THE FLY on a grand scale: human/insect gene-spliced body horror, where the human hive politics are as shocking as the gore." -John Skipp. **272 pages $13**

BB-093 "Sunset with a Beard" Carlton Mellick III — 14 stories of surreal science fiction. **200 pages $12**

BB-094 "My Fake War" Andersen Prunty — The absurd tale of an unlikely soldier forced to fight a war that, quite possibly, does not exist. It's Rambo meets Waiting for Godot in this subversive satire of American values and the scope of the human imagination. **128 pages $11**

BB-095 "Lost in Cat Brain Land" Cameron Pierce — Sad stories from a surreal world. A fascist mustache, the ghost of Franz Kafka, a desert inside a dead cat. Primordial entities mourn the death of their child. The desperate serve tea to mysterious creatures. A hopeless romantic falls in love with a pterodactyl. And much more. **152 pages $11**

BB-096 "The Kobold Wizard's Dildo of Enlightenment +2" Carlton Mellick III — A Dungeons and Dragons parody about a group of people who learn they are only made up characters in an AD&D campaign and must find a way to resist their nerdy teenaged players and retarded dungeon master in order to survive. 232 **pages $12**

BB-098 "A Hundred Horrible Sorrows of Ogner Stump" Andrew Goldfarb — Goldfarb's acclaimed comic series. A magical and weird journey into the horrors of everyday life. **164 pages $11**

BB-099 "Pickled Apocalypse of Pancake Island" Cameron Pierce—A demented fairy tale about a pickle, a pancake, and the apocalypse. 102 pages $8

BB-100 "Slag Attack" Andersen Prunty— Slag Attack features four visceral, noir stories about the living, crawling apocalypse.A slag is what survivors are calling the slug-like maggots raining from the sky, burrowing inside people, and hollowing out their flesh and their sanity. 148 pages $11

BB-101 "Slaughterhouse High" Robert Devereaux—A place where schools are built with secret passageways, rebellious teens get zippers installed in their mouths and genitals, and once a year, on that special night, one couple is slaughtered and the bits of their bodies are kept as souvenirs. 304 pages $13

BB-102 "The Emerald Burrito of Oz" John Skipp & Marc Levinthal —OZ IS REAL! Magic is real! The gate is really in Kansas! And America is finally allowing Earth tourists to visit this weird-ass, mysterious land. But when Gene of Los Angeles heads off for summer vacation in the Emerald City, little does he know that a war is brewing...a war that could destroy both worlds. 280 pages $13

BB-103 "The Vegan Revolution... with Zombies" David Agranoff — When there's no more meat in hell, the vegans will walk the earth. 160 pages $11

BB-104 "The Flappy Parts" Kevin L Donihe—Poems about bunnies, LSD, and police abuse. You know, things that matter. 132 pages $11

BB-105 "Sorry I Ruined Your Orgy" Bradley Sands—Bizarro humorist Bradley Sands returns with one of the strangest, most hilarious collections of the year. 130 pages $11

BB-106 "Mr. Magic Realism" Bruce Taylor—Like Golden Age science fiction comics written by Freud, Mr. Magic Realism is a strange, insightful adventure that spans the furthest reaches of the galaxy, exploring the hidden caverns in the hearts and minds of men, women, aliens, and biomechanical cats. 152 pages $11

BB-107 **"Zombies and Shit" Carlton Mellick III**—"Battle Royale" meets "Return of the Living Dead." Mellick's bizarro tribute to the zombie genre. **308 pages $13**

BB-108 **"The Cannibal's Guide to Ethical Living" Mykle Hansen**— Over a five star French meal of fine wine, organic vegetables and human flesh, a lunatic delivers a witty, chilling, disturbingly sane argument in favor of eating the rich.. **184 pages $11**

BB-109 **"Starfish Girl" Athena Villaverde**—In a post-apocalyptic underwater dome society, a girl with a starfish growing from her head and an assassin with sea anenome hair are on the run from a gang of mutant fish men. **160 pages $11**

BB-110 **"Lick Your Neighbor" Chris Genoa**—Mutant ninjas, a talking whale, kung fu masters, maniacal pilgrims, and an alcoholic clown populate Chris Genoa's surreal, darkly comical and unnerving reimagining of the first Thanksgiving. **303 pages $13**

BB-111 **"Night of the Assholes" Kevin L. Donihe**—A plague of assholes is infecting the countryside. Normal everyday people are transforming into jerks, snobs, dicks, and douchebags. And they all have only one purpose: to make your life a living hell.. **192 pages $11**

BB-112 **"Jimmy Plush, Teddy Bear Detective" Garrett Cook**—Hardboiled cases of a private detective trapped within a teddy bear body. **180 pages $11**

BB-113 **"The Deadheart Shelters" Forrest Armstrong**—The hip hop lovechild of William Burroughs and Dali... **144 pages $11**

BB-114 **"Eyeballs Growing All Over Me... Again" Tony Raugh**— Absurd, surreal, playful, dream-like, whimsical, and a lot of fun to read. **144 pages $11**

BB-115 "Whargoul" Dave Brockie — From the killing grounds of Stalingrad to the death camps of the holocaust. From torture chambers in Iraq to race riots in the United States, the Whargoul was there, killing and raping. **244 pages $12**

BB-116 "By the Time We Leave Here, We'll Be Friends" J. David Osborne — A David Lynchian nightmare set in a Russian gulag, where its prisoners, guards, traitors, soldiers, lovers, and demons fight for survival and their own rapidly deteriorating humanity. **168 pages $11**

BB-117 "Christmas on Crack" edited by Carlton Mellick III — Perverted Christmas Tales for the whole family! . . . as long as every member of your family is over the age of 18. **168 pages $11**

BB-118 "Crab Town" Carlton Mellick III — Radiation fetishists, balloon people, mutant crabs, sail-bike road warriors, and a love affair between a woman and an H-Bomb. This is one mean asshole of a city. Welcome to Crab Town. **100 pages $8**

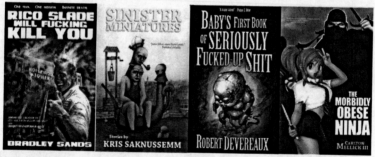

BB-119 "Rico Slade Will Fucking Kill You" Bradley Sands — Rico Slade is an action hero. Rico Slade can rip out a throat with his bare hands. Rico Slade's favorite food is the honey-roasted peanut. Rico Slade will fucking kill everyone. A novel. **122 pages $8**

BB-120 "Sinister Miniatures" Kris Saknussemm — The definitive collection of short fiction by Kris Saknussemm, confirming that he is one of the best, most daring writers of the weird to emerge in the twenty-first century. **180 pages $11**

BB-121 "Baby's First Book of Seriously Fucked up Shit" Robert Devereaux — Ten stories of the strange, the gross, and the just plain fucked up from one of the most original voices in horror. **176 pages $11**

BB-122 "The Morbidly Obese Ninja" Carlton Mellick III — These days, if you want to run a successful company . . . you're going to need a lot of ninjas. **92 pages $8**

BB-123 "Abortion Arcade" Cameron Pierce — An intoxicating blend of body horror and midnight movie madness, reminiscent of early David Lynch and the splatterpunks at their most sublime. **172 pages $11**

BB-124 "Black Hole Blues" Patrick Wensink — A hilarious double helix of country music and physics. **196 pages $11**

BB-125 "Barbarian Beast Bitches of the Badlands" Carlton Mellick III — Three prequels and sequels to *Warrior Wolf Women of the Wasteland*. **284 pages $13**

BB-126 "The Traveling Dildo Salesman" Kevin L. Donihe — A nightmare comedy about destiny, faith, and sex toys. Also featuring Donihe's most lurid and infamous short stories: *Milky Agitation, Two-Way Santa, The Helen Mower, Living Room Zombies,* and *Revenge of the Living Masturbation Rag.* **108 pages $8**

BB-127 "Metamorphosis Blues" Bruce Taylor — Enter a land of love beasts, intergalactic cowboys, and rock 'n roll. A land where Sears Catalogs are doorways to insanity and men keep mysterious black boxes. Welcome to the monstrous mind of Mr. Magic Realism. **136 pages $11**

BB-128 "The Driver's Guide to Hitting Pedestrians" Andersen Prunty — A pocket guide to the twenty-three most painful things in life, written by the most well-adjusted man in the universe. **108 pages $8**

BB-129 "Island of the Super People" Kevin Shamel — Four students and their anthropology professor journey to a remote island to study its indigenous population. But this is no ordinary native culture. They're super heroes and villains with flesh costumes and outlandish abilities like self-detonation, musical eyelashes, and microwave hands. **194 pages $11**

BB-130 "Fantastic Orgy" Carlton Mellick III — Shark Sex, mutant cats, and strange sexually transmitted diseases. Featuring the stories: *Candy-coated, Ear Cat, Fantastic Orgy, City Hobgoblins,* and *Porno in August.* **136 pages $9**

BB-131 "Cripple Wolf" Jeff Burk — Part man. Part wolf. 100% crippled. Also including *Punk Rock Nursing Home, Adrift with Space Badgers, Cook for Your Life, Just Another Day in the Park, Frosty and the Full Monty,* and *House of Cats.* **152 pages $10**

BB-132 "I Knocked Up Satan's Daughter" Carlton Mellick III — An adorable, violent, fantastical love story. A romantic comedy for the bizarro fiction reader. **152 pages $10**

BB-133 "A Town Called Suckhole" David W. Barbee — Far into the future, in the nuclear bowels of post-apocalyptic Dixie, there is a town. A town of derelict mobile homes, ancient junk, and mutant wildlife. A town of slack jawed rednecks who bask in the splendors of moonshine and mud boggin'. A town dedicated to the bloody and demented legacy of the Old South. A town called Suckhole. **144 pages $10**

BB-134 "Cthulhu Comes to the Vampire Kingdom" Cameron Pierce — What you'd get if H. P. Lovecraft wrote a Tim Burton animated film. **148 pages $11**

BB-135 "I am Genghis Cum" Violet LeVoit — From the savage Arctic tundra to post-partum mutations to your missing daughter's unmarked grave, join visionary madwoman Violet LeVoit in this non-stop eight-story onslaught of full-tilt Bizarro punk lit thrills. **124 pages $9**

BB-136 "Haunt" Laura Lee Bahr — A tripping-balls Los Angeles noir, where a mysterious dame drags you through a time-warping Bizarro hall of mirrors. **316 pages $13**

BB-137 "Amazing Stories of the Flying Spaghetti Monster" edited by Cameron Pierce — Like an all-spaghetti evening of Adult Swim, the Flying Spaghetti Monster will show you the many realms of His Noodly Appendage. Learn of those who worship him and the lives he touches in distant, mysterious ways. **228 pages $12**

BB-138 "Wave of Mutilation" Douglas Lain — A dream-pop exploration of modern architecture and the American identity, *Wave of Mutilation* is a Zen finger trap for the 21st century. **100 pages $8**

BB-139 **"Hooray for Death!" Mykle Hansen** — Famous Author Mykle Hansen draws unconventional humor from deaths tiny and large, and invites you to laugh while you can. **128 pages $10**

BB-140 **"Hypno-hog's Moonshine Monster Jamboree" Andrew Goldfarb** — Hicks, Hogs, Horror! Goldfarb is back with another strange illustrated tale of backwoods weirdness. **120 pages $9**

BB-141 **"Broken Piano For President" Patrick Wensink** — A comic masterpiece about the fast food industry, booze, and the necessity to choose happiness over work and security. **372 pages $15**

BB-142 **"Please Do Not Shoot Me in the Face" Bradley Sands** — A novel in three parts, *Please Do Not Shoot Me in the Face: A Novel*, is the story of one boy detective, the worst ninja in the world, and the great American fast food wars. It is a novel of loss, destruction, and--incredibly--genuine hope. **224 pages $12**

BB-143 **"Santa Steps Out" Robert Devereaux** — Sex, Death, and Santa Claus ... The ultimate erotic Christmas story is back. **294 pages $13**

BB-144 **"Santa Conquers the Homophobes" Robert Devereaux** — "I wish I could hope to ever attain one-thousandth the perversity of Robert Devereaux's toenail clippings." - Poppy Z. Brite **316 pages $13**

BB-145 **"We Live Inside You" Jeremy Robert Johnson** — "Jeremy Robert Johnson is dancing to a way different drummer. He loves language, he loves the edge, and he loves us people. These stories have range and style and wit. This is entertainment... and literature."- Jack Ketchum **188 pages $11**

BB-146 **"Clockwork Girl" Athena Villaverde** — Urban fairy tales for the weird girl in all of us. Like a combination of Francesca Lia Block, Charles de Lint, Kathe Koja, Tim Burton, and Hayao Miyazaki, her stories are cute, kinky, edgy, magical, provocative, and strange, full of poetic imagery and vicious sexuality. **160 pages $10**

BB-147 **"Armadillo Fists" Carlton Mellick III** — A weird-as-hell gangster story set in a world where people drive giant mechanical dinosaurs instead of cars. **168 pages $11**

BB-148 **"Gargoyle Girls of Spider Island" Cameron Pierce** — Four college seniors venture out into open waters for the tropical party weekend of a lifetime. Instead of a teenage sex fantasy, they find themselves in a nightmare of pirates, sharks, and sex-crazed monsters. **100 pages $8**

BB-149 **"The Handsome Squirm" by Carlton Mellick III** — Like Franz Kafka's *The Trial* meets an erotic body horror version of *The Blob*. **158 pages $11**

BB-150 **"Tentacle Death Trip" Jordan Krall** — It's *Death Race 2000* meets H. P. Lovecraft in bizarro author Jordan Krall's best and most suspenseful work to date. **224 pages $12**

BB-151 **"The Obese" Nick Antosca** — Like Alfred Hitchcock's *The Birds*... but with obese people. **108 pages $10**

BB-152 **"All-Monster Action!" Cody Goodfellow** — The world gave him a blank check and a demand: Create giant monsters to fight our wars. But Dr. Otaku was not satisfied with mere chaos and mass destruction.... **216 pages $12**

BB-153 **"Ugly Heaven" Carlton Mellick III** — Heaven is no longer a paradise. It was once a blissful utopia full of wonders far beyond human comprehension. But the afterlife is now in ruins. It has become an ugly, lonely wasteland populated by strange monstrous beasts, masturbating angels, and sad man-like beings wallowing in the remains of the once-great Kingdom of God. **106 pages $8**

BB-154 **"Space Walrus" Kevin L. Donihe** — Walter is supposed to go where no walrus has ever gone before, but all this astronaut walrus really wants is to take it easy on the intense training, escape the chimpanzee bullies, and win the love of his human trainer Dr. Stephanie. **160 pages $11**

BB-155 **"Unicorn Battle Squad" Kirsten Alene** — Mutant unicorns. A palace with a thousand human legs. The most powerful army on the planet. **192 pages $11**

BB-156 **"Kill Ball" Carlton Mellick III** — In a city where all humans live inside of plastic bubbles, exotic dancers are being murdered in the rubbery streets by a mysterious stalker known only as Kill Ball. **134 pages $10**

BB-157 **"Die You Doughnut Bastards" Cameron Pierce** — The bacon storm is rolling in. We hear the grease and sugar beat against the roof and windows. The doughnut people are attacking. We press close together, forgetting for a moment that we hate each other. **196 pages $11**

BB-158 **"Tumor Fruit" Carlton Mellick III** — Eight desperate castaways find themselves stranded on a mysterious deserted island. They are surrounded by poisonous blue plants and an ocean made of acid. Ravenous creatures lurk in the toxic jungle. The ghostly sound of crying babies can be heard on the wind. **310 pages $13**

BB-159 **"Thunderpussy" David W. Barbee** — When it comes to high-tech global espionage, only one man has the balls to save humanity from the world's most powerful bastards. He's Declan Magpie Bruce, Agent 00X. **136 pages $11**

BB-160 **"Papier Mâché Jesus" Kevin L. Donihe** — Donihe's surreal wit and beautiful mind-bending imagination is on full display with stories such as All Children Go to Hell, Happiness is a Warm Gun, and Swimming in Endless Night. **154 pages $11**

BB-161 **"Cuddly Holocaust" Carlton Mellick III** — The war between humans and toys has come to an end. The toys won. **172 pages $11**

BB-162 **"Hammer Wives" Carlton Mellick III** — Fish-eyed mutants, oceans of insects, and flesh-eating women with hammers for heads. Hammer Wives collects six of his most popular novelettes and short stories. **152 pages $10**

CPSIA information can be obtained at www.ICGtesting.com
Printed in the USA
LVOW08s0511161113

361559LV00001B/197/P